THE Artsy SMaRtsy CLUB

DANIEL PINKWATER

THE ARTSY SMARTSY CLUB

ILLUSTRATED BY
JILL PINKWATER

HARPERCOLLINSPUBLISHERS

Library of Congress Cataloging-in-Publication Data
Pinkwater, Daniel Manus, 1941–
   The Artsy Smartsy Club / by Daniel Pinkwater ;
illustrated by Jill Pinkwater.— 1st ed.
        p.   cm.
   Summary: After three Hoboken children and their giant
chicken Henrietta begin to appreciate beautiful sidewalk
art, they venture into art class and visits to Manhattan.
   ISBN 0-06-053557-1 — ISBN 0-06-053558-X (lib. bdg.)
   [1. Artists—Fiction. 2. Art museums—Fiction. 3. Clubs—
Fiction. 4. Chickens—Fiction. 5. New York—Fiction.
6. Humorous stories.] I. Pinkwater, Jill, ill. II. Title.
PZ7.P6335Arf 2005   2004014598
[Fic]—dc22

1 2 3 4 5 6 7 8 9 10

First Edition

To A. W. Alabaster, aka T.L.

The wind, the wind, the wind,
That I am, that am I,
My unseen wanderings,
Who can pursue,
Who can comprehend?
                    —*Albert Pinkham Ryder*

I believe it is impossible to
make sense of life in this world
except through art.
                    —*Daniel Pinkwater*

I

There's a point in the summer when things slow down. It's after the Hoboken Bat Hat Festival and the Fourth of July, and before Old Hoboken Days and the Italian street fair that comes just before school begins. The whole town seems to go slower, one day runs into the next, lots of people go away on vacation, and the streets are kind of empty. It feels like summer is going to go on forever, and my friends Loretta Fischetti and Bruno Ugg and I were caught in the middle of the slowness.

The library was closed. Our friend Starr Lackawanna, the librarian, was away on a kayaking holiday in Baffin Bay. Vic Trola, the pirate disc jockey, was visiting his mother in

Henfanger, Florida, and Radio Jolly Roger, the pirate radio station, was off the air while Vic Trola was away. This made the whole town seem strangely quiet. Everybody in Hoboken listens to that station.

My parents were busy prying up old linoleum, scraping woodwork, and trying to restore our 120-year-old house, something they'd probably be doing for the next twenty years. We weren't going to be taking a vacation or going on any weekend jaunts. Loretta Fischetti's and Bruno Ugg's families were busy working, and not planning any trips either. We were stuck in the city—all of us kids—with nothing in particular to do. We kicked around the streets. We read books in the basement of Loretta and Bruno's building. We took Henrietta to Tesev Noskecnil Park and played on the slide and the swings.

Henrietta is my giant chicken . . . six feet tall and 266 pounds. Henrietta isn't exactly my chicken. For a long time, she belonged to Arthur Bobowicz, better known as Vic Trola, his disc jockey name. Vic had her since he was a kid my age. But he got to be very busy running his pirate radio station and wasn't paying enough attention to Henrietta. This led to Henrietta going off by herself and getting into trouble.

Professor Mazzocchi, the mad scientist who had created Henrietta in the first place, suggested that Vic Trola sort of lend her to me—more or less permanently—I guess because he noticed how much Henrietta and I liked each other. It's just the same as though she were really my chicken. I wouldn't have it any other way.

We were on our own—three kids and a giant chicken. We did a fair amount of exploring. We hiked along the streets, visiting every block and every alley in town. We watched the trains and saw tugboats come in and out at the dock next to the railroad station. We spat in the Hudson River. We were starting to get bored. We really really needed to find something, something interesting.

We were wandering around down by the railroad station, feeding marshmallows to Henrietta. Henrietta loves marshmallows, and she has a special way of eating them— we toss a marshmallow up over her head, and she catches it on the tip of her beak, then she bounces it—once, twice, three times—before gobbling it down. The plan is to teach her to juggle three marshmallows, but we haven't worked out exactly how to do it.

"The problem is, she keeps eating them," Loretta Fischetti said.

"Maybe we could switch to something she can't eat," Bruno Ugg said. "Like golf balls."

"Only then she might get confused and swallow a golf ball," I said.

"True," Bruno Ugg said. "That couldn't be good for her."

We were walking along as we talked, tossing marshmallows to Henrietta. Just as we got to the statue of Sam Sloan, Loretta Fischetti saw something amazing.

"Look at that!" Loretta Fischetti said, pointing down at the pavement.

Someone had drawn a picture with colored chalks. It was more than a picture—it was like a painting. The colors were sort of magical, and it didn't seem flat—you could look deep into it. Around the picture there was a fancy gold frame, done in chalk, with loops and curls. A real artist had done it, that was obvious.

But what was really amazing was the subject of the picture. It was a big white chicken, bouncing a marshmallow on its beak! It was Henrietta!

"How do you suppose that got there?" I asked.

"Obviously someone drew it," Loretta Fischetti said.

"It must have been some fast drawer," Bruno Ugg said.

"You think that someone saw us and drew this picture just now, while we were over there by the station?" Loretta Fischetti asked.

"What else is there to think?" Bruno Ugg asked. "Whoever did this got the marshmallow and everything. I wonder where they went."

"I don't think you can draw a picture like this in a couple of minutes," I said.

"Look, we are always around with Henrietta, and we toss marshmallows to her all the time," Loretta Fischetti said. "Obviously the person who drew the picture has seen us and did the picture, but not before yesterday."

"You mean did it from memory?" Bruno Ugg asked. "That impresses me even more."

"Why not before yesterday?" I asked Loretta Fischetti.

"Because it rained yesterday," Loretta Fischetti said. "The rain would have washed away the chalk."

"It's a really good picture," Bruno Ugg said. "I wish we could take it with us."

"So do I," Loretta Fischetti said.

"It's a really good picture," I said.

III

Loretta Fischetti and Bruno Ugg live in the apartment building next door to my house. Their basement is sort of our clubhouse. We usually wander in, one by one, sometime after breakfast. We might read, or talk, or listen to cowboy songs and blues on the old radio—when Vic Trola is in town and Radio Jolly Roger is on the air. When we go out to do things, Loretta Fischetti and Bruno Ugg's basement is where we start, and when we come back, that's where we wind up.

The morning after the day we found the chalk drawing of Henrietta, I was the first one to arrive. I had grabbed an oatmeal cookie, a slice of cold pizza, and a glass of milk; given Henrietta her morning chicken kibble; and headed for the basement next door while my parents were still brushing their teeth. I figured it would be at least an hour before Loretta Fischetti and Bruno Ugg showed up, and there was something I wanted to do.

I had dug out my old Junior Artist sketchbook and a box of thirty-two crayons, most of them with the points still pointy. I settled down on the old couch—Henrietta curled up at the other end. I flipped open the sketchbook and got to work.

It was a picture of Henrietta. I was trying to do it like the chalk drawing we had seen, with red drapes behind and to one side of Henrietta, and clouds in a blue sky in the distance. The time flashed by. . . . I must have been drawing for an hour, and it seemed like a minute, when I heard someone coming down the stairs. Henrietta gave a cluck that was in between "Hello" and "Warning! There's someone coming." Henrietta is a great watchchicken.

I slid the sketchbook under the couch and stuffed the crayons into their box, which I slid behind a cushion. I wasn't sure why I didn't want the other kids to see what I was doing, but I didn't. Probably I was afraid they would think I was silly.

I didn't have to worry. Loretta Fischetti was clunking down the stairs with a whole easel—the kind they have in kindergarten, with five jars of poster paint arranged in little holes along the bottom.

"Where'd you get that?" I asked Loretta Fischetti.

"Saved it from when I was little," she said. "I'm going to do some painting."

"I brought crayons and a sketchbook," I said, bringing them out.

"Cool," Loretta Fischetti said. After giving Henrietta a good-morning head scratch, she unfolded her easel. She had to sit on a milk crate to be at the right height to paint on it, because it was little-kid-sized. Loretta Fischetti started in on her own version of the Henrietta picture.

Bruno Ugg turned up. "What's this? Baby art class?" he asked.

"Was Rembrandt a baby?" Loretta Fischetti asked. "Was Picasso a baby? Was . . . what's the name of another famous artist?"

I couldn't think of one.

"Beethoven?" Bruno Ugg suggested.

"He did music, not art," Loretta Fischetti said.

"Anyway, I only meant that you are using baby art supplies," Bruno Ugg said. "Whereas, I have"—he produced a slim metal box from his pocket—"genuine professional watercolors."

"Oh, yes, I see you have the Happy Kitten brand, favored by great painters of the past," Loretta Fischetti said.

"I need a sheet of paper," Bruno Ugg said.

I tore a page from my Junior Artist sketchbook.

"Here," I said. "Knock yourself out."

We labored away at our pictures. There was no sound in the basement but our breathing and Henrietta's quiet snoring. Time passed.

"Mine's finished," Bruno Ugg said.

"Mine too," Loretta Fischetti said.

"I've gone about as far as I can go with this one," I said.

We taped our pictures to the wall and looked at them.

"They're good," Bruno Ugg said.

"In a crummy way," I said.

"But they're not like the picture on the pavement," Loretta Fischetti said.

"No," Bruno Ugg said. "Nowhere near."

"Let's go and look at that picture again," I said.

At the words "Let's go," Henrietta woke up and was on her feet.

"Good idea," Loretta Fischetti said. "Let's go."

Henrietta headed for the stairs, and we hurried after her.

When we got to the statue of Sam Sloan, the picture of Henrietta bouncing a marshmallow was still there, a little scuffed. It looked like a pedestrian or two, and maybe a dog, had walked across it—probably at night, when they wouldn't have seen they were walking on a picture ... except the dog, of course—the dog might have walked on it at any time. But it was mostly intact.

After trying to do Henrietta pictures of our own, we were able to see how really good the sidewalk picture was. We looked at it for a long time, noticing neat things the artist had done.

"That's how you draw an eye!" Loretta Fischetti said. "The eye in my painting stinks."

"I was just thinking, I want to do another one and do the feathers more like this,"

Bruno Ugg said.

"Look over here," I said. "There's another picture!" I had discovered another chalk drawing over near the iron fence.

Loretta Fischetti and Bruno Ugg hurried over to look at the picture. It showed a bunch of ballet dancers standing around wearing those fluffy ballet skirts—I didn't know what they were called.

"Tutus," Loretta Fischetti said.

"Too-toos?" Bruno Ugg asked. "Too-too what?"

"A tutu is what you call one of those ballet skirts," Loretta Fischetti said.

The skirts were all different pastel colors, and the dancers were standing in different positions, and they were all . . . chickens.

"Is this by the same artist?" Bruno Ugg asked. "It's a whole different . . ."

"Style," Loretta Fishetti said. "It's a different style. But I think it is by the same artist. Look how the chickens are drawn—sort of like Henrietta in the other picture."

"The feathers are good," Bruno Ugg said.

"There's another picture over here," I said.

There was another picture a little way along the fence. We gathered around it.

"Ohhh," Loretta Fischetti said.

"Ohhh," Bruno Ugg said.

"Wow," I said.

This was the best picture yet. It showed a little village along the bottom, with dark hills behind it, but most of the picture was the night sky. There was a crescent moon, surrounded by a circle of pale yellow light. There were clouds—or maybe it was mist—sort of rolling across the sky. And there were big glowing stars, more like little moons or suns, glowing yellow, green, and blue and white. In front of everything and to the left, there was a dark, scraggly something—a bush, or a tree, or a chicken. The thing about this picture was . . . it was like the sky was swirling, moving, tumbling.

"This is great," I said.

"This is the best picture I ever saw," Loretta Fishetti said.

"I want to be an artist," Bruno Ugg said.

"So do I."

"I do too."

"**C**luck!" Henrietta said.

Plop! A fat raindrop hit the wonderful picture.

Splat! Another one fell.

Plop! Splat! Plop!

"Oh, no! It's raining!" Bruno Ugg said.

Plop! Plop! Splat! Plop, plop, plop, plop-plop-plop.

We saw the colors spread and run and disappear as the raindrops washed the chalk off the pavement. We stood there, getting wet, and watched the magical starry night disappear, slowly at first, and then faster, until there was nothing but sidewalk, darkened with rain.

We didn't say anything as we walked home,

soaking wet. It was sad seeing the pictures wiped out—but at the same time, I was seeing them in my mind, and trying not to let go of them.

VII

We were heading for our basement, but Bruno Ugg's mother caught us. Mrs. Ugg. She insisted that we go to our respective homes and put on dry clothes. Our plan had been to put our clothes in the dryer that was right there in the basement and paint in our under-wear. We wanted to get started while those stars were still fresh in our minds.

Mrs. Ugg said that standing around in our underwear was indecent, and besides, wear-ing soggy underwear was absolutely certain to give us all colds, and probably flu and pneumonia. We suggested that we could put our underwear in the dryer too, and paint in the nude.

"If you kids turn nudist, I am going to lock

you out of here," Mrs. Ugg said. "No one wants naked children in the basement."

So we raced off to change into dry things, and were back in five minutes. Mrs. Ugg brought us mugs of hot chocolate and oatmeal cookies, and we munched as we painted and drew.

It rained all day. We made a lot of art. We did stars and chickens in tutus and chickens and stars and portraits of Henrietta. Henrietta was a good model, if you wanted to paint a picture called *The Sleeping Chicken*. We could get her to strike more interesting poses, but once we ran out of oatmeal cookies she lost interest, and napped.

After a while we started running out of art supplies.

"We need more stuff," Loretta Fischetti said.

"And better stuff," Bruno Ugg said. "I wonder where we can get some chalks like the sidewalk artist uses."

"And big paper," I said. "This Junior Artist sketchbook is too small."

"We can see if Sean Vergessen has any art supplies—or maybe the drugstore," Loretta Fischetti said.

"We could," I said. "But it will be more dinky kiddie art stuff. Where do you suppose real artists get their stuff?"

"How about Dave's Paint and Hardware?" Bruno Ugg suggested.

"Good suggestion!" I said. "Do we have any money?"

"Not particularly," Loretta Fischetti said.

"I have money," Bruno Ugg said. "I have money I am saving to buy Christmas presents."

"Oh, I have Christmas present money too," I said.

"So, do I," Loretta Fischetti said. "But should we spend it on art supplies?"

"Well, look," I said. "I think we are doing some pretty nice art, don't you agree?"

"I agree," Bruno Ugg said. "And we've only just started being artists."

"Exactly," I said. "It stands to reason that we are going to get much better. Pretty soon we will be turning out great pictures."

"Ohhh! I get it!" Loretta Fischetti said. "If we spend our Christmas present savings on art supplies, and make lots of good pictures—"

"We can give everybody art when Christmas rolls around," I said.

"Nick, that is a genius idea," Bruno Ugg said.

Nick is my name. At least, that's what everyone calls me. It's my nickname. Nick is my nickname. My actual name is Ivan . . . Ivan Itch. I prefer being called Nick.

My parents were happy. They said the damp air made it easier to strip wallpaper. For them, scraping old wallpaper off the walls is better than a trip to the Grand Canyon.

"Are you sure you don't want to help us peel wallpaper, old bean?" my father asked me. "It's jolly good fun."

My father talks like that.

"I'd love to have fun helping you strip a hundred and twenty years' worth of moldy wallpaper," I said. "But I'm doing stuff with my friends right now."

"I am so glad we made the decision to leave the suburbs," my mother said. "Our boy is doing stuff with his friends—his urban friends. He is having a rich and sophisticated life in a city."

"I am," I said. "Currently we are learning about art."

"You hear that?" my mother asked my father. "He's learning about art. If we had stayed in Happy Valley, I doubt he would have been learning about art."

"Quite so, old girl," my father said. "This place is a hotbed of culture—no doubt about it."

"I was wondering if you could advance me some money," I asked my father.

"I suppose something could be arranged," my father said. "But I'll need to know what it is for."

"Well, it has to do with Christmas presents," I said. "Indirectly."

"Thinking of Christmas presents now, in the middle of the summer?" my father asked.

"Indirectly," I said.

"Well, I won't pry into your doings," my father said. "I suppose I can let you have a few spondulix."

Spondulix is money. Hanging around with my father as long as I have, one starts to sort of know what he's talking about.

IX

With the money my father gave me added to what I had already saved, I had a fat wad of spondulix. Bruno Ugg and Loretta Fischetti had been gathering funds too, and when we met outside our side-by-side buildings, we were ready to get ourselves outfitted as artists.

"Let's go to Dave's Paint and Hardware and see what they have," Loretta Fischetti said.

They had nothing at all.

"Art supplies are a whole different category," Dave told us.

I knew Dave pretty well, because my parents were constantly sending me to get house-renovating things—wallpaper scrapers, sandpaper, cans of varnish—things of that kind.

"You have to go to an art supplies specialist,"

Dave told us. "I suggest you visit Davis Davisdavis Fine Art Supplies."

"Where is it?" we asked.

"It's right at Twenty-third Street and Sixth Avenue," Dave said. "When you come up the stairs from the tube station, you'll be right in front of the building. I think it's on the fifth floor."

"It's in New York? Manhattan?" we asked.

"Sure," Dave said.

"Twenty-third Street and Sixth Avenue?"

"Right."

"And we just come up the stairs from the tubes, and we're there?"

"Yep."

"Fifth floor?"

"I think so. There will be a directory next to the elevator."

"Thanks, Dave."

"Think nothing of it."

We stood in the street in front of Dave's Paint and Hardware.

"Are you allowed to go into Manhattan?" I asked Loretta Fischetti and Bruno Ugg.

"Not by myself," Bruno Ugg said.

"Me neither," Loretta Fischetti said.

"But you've been there, haven't you?" I asked.

"Oh, several times," Bruno Ugg said. "How about you?"

"Twice," I said.

"And you're allowed to go by yourself?" Loretta Fischetti asked.

"Actually, it's never come up," I said. "No one ever said I couldn't."

"So . . . technically, if we went to Manhattan with you . . . ," Bruno Ugg said.

"We wouldn't be going by ourselves," Loretta Fischetti said.

"And Davis Davisdavis Fine Art Supplies is right there," Bruno Ugg said. "We'd just get off the train, get our stuff, and take the train right back."

"It would hardly be like leaving Hoboken at all," I said.

"Let's go."

We left Henrietta in the basement with the radio playing and some chicken kibble to snack on, and headed for the tubes.

X

The tubes is what people call the subway trains that run from Hoboken to New York City. Actually, I guess the tunnels are the tubes—the trains are called PATH, for Port Authority Trans Hudson. They go under the Hudson River, and it takes about fifteen minutes to get to Twenty-third Street.

We went down the flight of stairs, paid our fares, and got onto a train. We sat there for a while, watching people get on. Then the doors whooshed shut, and we felt the electric engines vibrate. The train began to move! A voice over a loudspeaker said, "This is the PATH train to New York City—stopping at Christopher Street, Ninth Street, Fourteenth Street, Twenty-third Street, Thirty-third Street."

Loretta Fischetti counted on her fingers,

"Christopher, Ninth, Fourteenth, Twenty-third. The fourth stop is ours."

Outside the train was complete blackness. We could see our reflections in the windows across from us.

"We're underneath the Hudson River," I said.

"Neat!" Bruno Ugg said.

"There are tons of water on top of us, and tugboats, and fish, and mud, and dead bodies," Loretta Fischetti said.

"Dead bodies?" I asked.

"Sure," Loretta Fischetti said. "People drown in the river and float around up there."

"Neat!" Bruno Ugg said.

"And thirty-four workmen died building the tunnels," Loretta Fischetti said. "Some of them are still down here, encased in concrete."

"How do you know all this?" I asked.

"Studied it in school," Loretta Fischetti said. "Oh, and there are sharks in the river."

"Neat!" Bruno Ugg said.

"It's salty," Loretta Fischetti said.

"What, the river?" I asked.

"Yep. It's salty for about eighty miles up.

It's sort of part ocean and part river."

"Big sharks?" I asked.

"Sure," Loretta Fischetti said. "They eat the dead bodies."

"I love the Hudson River!" Bruno Ugg said.

"The station is Christopher Street," the voice on the loudspeaker said.

"One," we all said.

The train came to a stop, the doors whooshed open, and some people got out. Then the doors whooshed shut, and we were moving again.

"Next stop is Ninth Street. Ninth Street," the voice said.

"Two," we all said.

As the train left Fourteenth Street, Loretta Fischetti said, "We'd better stand by the doors."

We got up and stood by the doors, holding on to the chrome poles.

"Twenty-third Street. Twenty-third Street."

The doors opened, and we stepped out onto the platform.

"We're in New York," Bruno Ugg said.

"There are the stairs," I said.

"Let's go," Loretta Fischetti said.

XI

As we made our way up the stairs, the first thing we saw was sky, then the tops of buildings, then more of the buildings, then more and more, and then . . . we were on the sidewalk. Buses, cars, and people, people, people— the intersection of Sixth Avenue and Twenty-third Street looked bigger than all of Hoboken. And it smelled different—exhaust fumes, sweat, perfume, and onions and peppers cooking. And there was noise. New York rumbles and growls and screeches and honks. And the light is different. The air is different. It made me feel a little dizzy and scared. Part of me wanted to run down the stairs and get back onto a train—but part of me was excited.

"This must be the building," Bruno Ugg said.

We went in. There was a little lobby that smelled of cigar smoke. There were two elevator doors, and on the wall, framed in shiny metal and covered with glass, was the building directory, white plastic letters stuck to fuzzy-looking black stuff—the names of the different people and companies in alphabetical order. Davis Davisdavis—fifth. We were in the right place. Elevator doors opened, and people got out. We got in and pressed five.

On the fifth floor, there was a little hallway. At the end was a black door, with a sign: DAVIS DAVISDAVIS FINE ART SUPPLIES. When we opened the door, we found a little space, not much bigger than the elevator we had just gotten out of. There was a counter, and beyond it a huge room with a high ceiling. It was full of high shelves, like the stacks in the library, but much higher. Someone was bustling around among the shelves, and a couple of people were standing in the little elevator-sized space. It was clear how the place worked. Customers would stand in front of the counter, and someone would take their order and

bring them what they wanted.

"What do we ask for?" I asked Loretta Fischetti and Bruno Ugg.

"I don't know . . . art stuff," Bruno Ugg said.

"The whole place is full of art stuff," I said.

"I am Davis Davisdavis," we heard someone shout. "This is not some shop, sir! I am a specialist! I am not some clerk—I am a purveyor of the finest materials. If you disagree with my choices, you do not belong here. Leave my establishment, sir, and never return!"

The guy doing the shouting was a little bald-headed man. He was kicking out a guy in a Hawaiian shirt and sunglasses.

"I only said I prefer Grumbacher oil paints," the guy in the shirt said.

"Grumbacher! I can't talk to you, sir. We don't speak the same language. Vanish! Disappear! Go to Macy's! Go to Gimbels! Go to the five-and-ten-cent store! You disgust me!"

The guy in the shirt turned to go.

"Wait!" Davis Davisdavis shouted. "I give you another chance. How will you learn if I don't educate you?" Davis Davisdavis held up a metal tube, like a toothpaste tube. "These colors are made by hand in Spain, by the same family that made paints for Velasquez, El Greco, Goya, and Picasso. The finest artists in Europe get all the colors they make, except one box—one box a year comes to the United States, and I have it. You want it or not?"

"Yes, yes, please, thank you," the guy in the shirt said.

"I'm wrapping them up," Davis Davisdavis said. "Brushes! You need brushes!"

"I . . . I have brushes," the shirt guy said.

"Not these brushes, you don't," Davis Davisdavis said. "Only I have these brushes. In a tiny village in China, a single family possesses the secret of great brushes. They raise special pigs just for their bristles. These pigs live indoors with the family, and are treated like their own children. They carefully shave the bristles, when the pigs are two years old, and fit them, one hair at a time, into brushes of exquisite quality. It takes a year to make each brush. A year! I have them, and they cost five ninety-nine each. I will give you five, in assorted sizes, for twenty bucks. You will thank me to your dying day."

Davis Davisdavis wrapped up the brushes and paints, and the shirt guy gave him money, and went out the door.

"This stuff is expensive," I whispered to Bruno Ugg and Loretta Fischetti. "Maybe we came to the wrong place."

"Children! Don't move a muscle!" Davis Davisdavis shouted. "I will tend to you after I have dealt with this customer. *Don't move!*"

We huddled together near the door, not moving.

The next customer was wearing a cape and had the longest, thinnest black moustache I ever saw. It stuck out three inches past his cheeks on either side.

"Thee grrreat artiste weeshes thee watercolorssssss," the guy in the cape said in a high, piping voice.

"Certainly, Maestro," Davis Davisdavis said. "Do you desire the ones from Madagascar, or the ones from Peru?"

Davis Davisdavis did not shout at this customer—he spoke sweetly, and sort of bowed.

"Thee grrreat artiste weeshes thee onesss from Tibet," the guy in the cape said. When he said the word "Tibet," his voice went up as high as a whistle.

"A superb choice, Maestro," Davis Davisdavis said. "They are made by the holy monks, as you know—and I have them in a special box made of bubinga wood from Africa."

Davis Davisdavis bowed low, as the grrreat artiste swirled his cape and went out the door, with his bubinga wood box of Tibetan watercolors.

XII

"**N**ow, children, how may I serve you?" Davis Davisdavis asked us.

"We're just beginners," I said.

"We aren't sure what we need," Bruno Ugg said.

"We don't need anything from Tibet," Loretta Fischetti said.

"Davis Davisdavis understands," Davis Davisdavis said. "Davis Davisdavis *knows*! I have a special department. Come, children. Come behind the counter. Follow Davis Davisdavis."

Davis Davisdavis reached over the counter and swung open a little door. We hesitated for a moment, then ducked under the counter and followed him through the rows of high shelves, which wobbled and swayed.

It was like going through a forest. Davis Davisdavis led us to a little clearing, near the windows. There were large open cartons, full of all sort of things.

"In this box, you will find brushes—a nickel a throw. They are domestic, but of good student quality—you may have to trim them with scissors. Here are watercolors in big cakes, poster paints in plastic jars, crayons, pencils, pastel chalks—nothing over twenty-five cents."

"Chalks! Are those the sort of chalks you can draw on the sidewalk with?" Loretta Fischetti asked.

"No, these are pastels. I recommend them. For sidewalk art you need the big lecturer's chalks. Davis Davisdavis has them. I supply the great screevers."

"Screevers?" we asked.

"Pavement artists," Davis Davisdavis said. "Even the famous Lucy Casserole uses my chalks."

"Who is Lucy Casserole?" we asked.

"She is a great, great screever," Davis Davisdavis said. "But the big chalks are expensive. Fifty cents apiece. Take the pastels for now; they're twenty for a dollar."

"We need big paper," I said.

"Davis Davisdavis has it!" Davis Davisdavis said. "You have heard of oatmeal paper?"

"The stuff they give you in kindergarten?"

"Only mine is made of real oatmeal," Davis Davisdavis said. "It's edible. And the pastels are nontoxic, so you can eat your pictures, if you get hungry. You'll take a roll of a hundred sheets. Come back when they're gone—Davis Davisdavis bought a whole carload."

"These nickel brushes look like the special Chinese pig bristle ones," Loretta Fischetti said.

"A superficial resemblance," Davis Davisdavis said. "But they're a good value. Davis Davisdavis will make up boxes with everything you need, and I am throwing in three genuine artists' berets—size small—at no charge."

We put the genuine artists' berets on our heads. They were little black hats with a noodle on top. Then we noticed something pinned to the wall.

"Look," Bruno Ugg said. "It's the picture of the starry night!"

"This is a print—a copy—of a painting by someone who lived in France," Davis Davisdavis said. He pulled the picture off the wall, and rolled it up. "Davis Davisdavis will throw it in too, also free."

"Wow, thanks," we said. "It's our favorite picture."

"Vincent, the artist who made this, wore a beret exactly like yours," Davis Davisdavis said.

In a little while, we were back in the street, staggering under the weight of three boxes full of art supplies and a huge roll of edible oatmeal paper. We were sweating under our genuine artists' berets, and some of the dye was running down our cheeks as we descended the stairs to catch the PATH train back to Hoboken.

We spent the rest of the day rummaging in my basement, which was full of 120 years' worth of assorted junk, and dragging things next door to Bruno Ugg and Loretta Fischetti's basement.

We found some floor lamps without shades, a real artist's easel, some big pieces of plywood, and three wobbly kitchen chairs. By putting the chairs against the wall, with one of the pieces of plywood on the seats, leaning against the wall, we had good places to pin the big pieces of edible oatmeal paper.

Bruno Ugg took a bite out of one of the pieces of paper and said it might be edible, but it wasn't tasty.

We also found some big pieces of thick

cardboard and a couple of little tables that would be good for holding paints and brushes and things.

It was almost suppertime when we had everything in our basement studio, and had gotten everything dusted off and arranged. The last thing we did was pin up the starry night picture Davis Davisdavis had given us.

"Davis Davisdavis said someone named Vincent did this," Bruno Ugg said.

"Gogh," Loretta Fischetti said.

"Gog?" Bruno Ugg asked.

"Spelled with an *H*," Loretta Fischetti said. "I assume the *H* is silent. His middle name is Van. See? Vincent Van Gogh. It's printed at the bottom."

"So this copy," I said. "Did they take a picture of the picture that Vincent did, and print that, or did someone actually copy it by hand?"

"The one we saw on the sidewalk was done by hand, and it's better than this one," Bruno Ugg said.

"I think it's better too," I said.

"It's bigger, for one thing," Loretta Fischetti said.

"And it's more ... more alive, sort of," I said.

"I think that's because it's a real picture, and this is a copy," Bruno Ugg said. "If we saw the one by Vincent, in person, I bet it would be better than this here one."

"Do you think Vincent did the one in chalk that we saw on the pavement?" I asked.

"Davis Davisdavis said he lives in France," Loretta Fischetti said.

"I'm going to do one tomorrow," I said.

"I was thinking the same thing," Bruno Ugg said.

"So was I," said Loretta Fischetti.

"We're not going to paint tonight?" Bruno Ugg asked. "We've got all these lights."

"We still have to steal lightbulbs from our houses," Loretta Fischetti said. "And we're pretty tired after all the stuff we did today. I say we start early tomorrow morning."

"Do we mention anything to our parents about going into Manhattan?"

"No."

XIV

"It's not Gog," I said when I came into the basement in the morning. "It's Gok, or more like Gockgh—like you're trying to clear your throat—and it's Van Gockgh, Vincent Van *G-o-g-h*, pronounced Van Gockgh."

"How do you know this?" Loretta Fischetti asked.

"My father told me."

"He just happened to tell you?"

"No, I asked him if he ever heard of an artist named Gog, and he figured out I meant Van Gogh. He's famous. He painted sunflowers."

"He painted sunflowers?"

"Yep, and he sliced his ear off."

"What do you mean, sliced his ear off?"

"My father said. He sliced his ear off and

sent it to a woman of the town."

"What, as a practical joke?" Bruno Ugg asked.

"I don't know," I said.

"He did it for love," Loretta Fischetti said.

Bruno Ugg and I looked at her.

"Where did you get that?" Bruno Ugg asked.

"It stands to reason," Loretta Fischetti said. "He was sensitive. He was in love with this woman who lived in the town, and when she rejected him, he got depressed and sliced his ear off."

Bruno Ugg and I looked at each other.

"Wow! So he was a looney tune!" Bruno Ugg said.

"Vincent Van Gogh is my favorite artist for all time."

"He was tragic," Loretta Fischetti said. "I bet he was handsome."

"My father said he used to hang around in poolrooms and annoy people," I said.

"He was a good artist," Loretta Fischetti said.

"Hey," Bruno Ugg said. "If you pull your

artist's beret down on one side, you can cover where you chopped off your ear. Look at me, I'm Vincent Van Gogh."

"So, I guess that's a French name," Loretta Fischetti said.

"I guess."

"I'm getting started copying this copy of this painting by good old Vincent," Bruno Ugg said.

"Yes, let's do that," I said.

We started with the paints. It wasn't so easy trying to copy the picture. For one thing, it turned out there was a trick to keeping the colors from all running together and looking like mud.

Our first few tries were completely awful. They turned into soggy messes, and we wound up stuffing them into the big waste-basket we had dragged over from my basement.

"I'm switching to the pastel chalks," I said.

"Good idea," Loretta Fischetti said.

Things went a little better with the chalks. We did some interesting pictures, but none of them looked a whole lot like Vincent's picture.

Then Bruno Ugg made a breakthrough. He did a picture of Henrietta that looked a little bit as though Vincent might have done it. He had drawn Henrietta in little short strokes and squiggles of chalk, and her eye looked like one of the stars in our print.

"I call this masterpiece *Starry Chicken*," Bruno Ugg said.

"You know, that's actually pretty good," I said.

"It is," Loretta Fischetti said. "But it's hard to make any progress copying this Vincent copy. I wish we could see the chalk one again."

"The chalk one is gone—washed away," I said. "And it rained a little the next day, and the day after that."

"It's not raining today," Bruno Ugg said.

"The sun is shining, and Henrietta needs some exercise," Loretta Fischetti said. "Let's go out and see if we can find some sidewalk art."

When we got to the big open space outside the railroad station, we found no chalk pictures. There weren't even any people around— just the statue of Sam Sloan and Jolly Roger, the famous dog.

Jolly Roger is the most famous dog in Hoboken—in fact, he is the most famous personality in Hoboken. He could get elected mayor, if he wanted to be mayor, but it doesn't seem likely that he would want to be mayor. Being mayor just wouldn't be important to a dog like Jolly Roger.

Jolly Roger is a celebrity just because of who he is, and the way he is. He's a medium-sized, mostly black dog, with some brown. His fur is curly, and his tail is curly. He's on the stocky side, with a short, wide muzzle and fat feet. What he looks most like is a Chinese Chow Chow—and he is certainly partly that kind of dog, with maybe some husky mixed in.

Technically, he belongs to this guy who is known as "The Kid," but really he belongs to himself. He goes all over town, and has a great many friends. But he isn't what you'd call a friendly dog. He is aloof. He ignores most people—and it's a big honor if Jolly Roger pays any attention to someone. Everyone talks to him, and people offer him treats, in hope of getting him to respond. If anyone gets a single tail wag from Jolly Roger, that person is all happy, and mentions to everybody that Jolly Roger is a friend of his. If Jolly Roger chooses to hang out with someone, that is considered the coolest thing that can possibly happen.

The dogs of Hoboken regard Jolly Roger as their king. They crawl up to him, like puppies, and give him little kisses. Actual puppies crowd around him and roll on their backs, waving their feet in the air. Jolly Roger likes puppies, and he will bump them with his nose and bat them playfully with his paws.

If Jolly Roger doesn't like a dog, that dog leaves town.

It's not that Jolly Roger does anything special most of the time—it's just that he *is* special. He's the king—he knows it, and everybody else knows it. He knows how to escape the dogcatcher, and he knows how to make a warm nest out of newspapers. The Hoboken dogs follow Jolly Roger and do whatever he does, and the Hoboken people bring him food, which the other dogs don't touch until Jolly Roger gives them permission.

Sometimes Jolly Roger walks aboard one of the tugboats that tie up next to the railroad station, and spends the day on the river. The crews of the tugboats give him sandwiches and holler to the other tugs, "Hey! We've got Jolly Roger on board!"

Jolly Roger sometimes will walk into a restaurant, or a barbershop, or the police station, and hang out for a while. And sometimes he gets into the car of this rich guy who works in Hoboken and lives on a big estate in the country. Jolly will go home with the rich guy and spend the weekend. On Monday the rich guy brings him back. And you are likely to see Jolly Roger in every neighborhood in town, visiting his friends. If Jolly Roger could write, people would ask for his autograph.

So, there was Jolly Roger, sitting quietly and gazing off into the distance, not far from the statue of Sam Sloan, when we came along, looking for sidewalk drawings.

There is one other thing about Jolly Roger that needs to be mentioned. Jolly Roger *loves* Henrietta. He is simply nuts about her. And Henrietta loves Jolly Roger. When she saw him sitting near the statue of Sam Sloan, she broke into a run. She charged right up to him. Jolly Roger saw her coming and began to bark, with his forepaws flat on the ground, his hind end up in the air, and his tail wagging. Then Jolly Roger and Henrietta danced around and chased each other—Jolly Roger barking and Henrietta clucking. There is no one Jolly

Roger likes more than Henrietta, and naturally that makes Loretta Fischetti, and Bruno Ugg, and especially me, very proud.

When we made our way up River Street, looking for sidewalk pictures, Jolly Roger trotted along with us.

XVI

At the top of River Street is Tesev Noskecnil Park, named after a famous walrus hunter from the earliest days of Hoboken. Henrietta headed straight for the children's playground—she loves the swings and the slides. Jolly Roger scampered after her, and met another one of his friends.

It was a little old lady in a flowered dress, wearing high-heeled shoes and kneepads.

"Why, hello, Jolly," the little old lady said.

Jolly Roger was on his back, waving his legs in the air, with a silly smile on his face. The little old lady bent over and scratched his belly.

"Aren't you a remarkable doggie?" the old lady said. "I think I may have a cookie for you in my bag."

She dug around in a big bag, which looked like it was made of a piece of carpet, with wooden handles at the top. She came up with a cookie, which she held up over Jolly Roger's head.

"Sit up, Jolly!" the little old lady said. "Beg for the cookie!"

This was astonishing. Jolly Roger sat up, put his paws together as though he were praying, and pumped them up and down—just as though he were an ordinary dog. We couldn't believe our eyes. Even Henrietta, who was standing on the seat of a swing, rocking back and forth, looked a little surprised.

"Who's a good boy?" the little old lady said. "Here is your cookie. And would your friend like a cookie?"

By this time Henrietta had trotted over to the little old lady.

"Ohhh, the dear chicken!" the little old lady said. She stood on tiptoe and scratched Henrietta's head. Then she dug out a cookie and gave it to her.

"Such nice animals!" the little old lady said.

Then to us she said, "And such nice children, all wearing berets. I am sorry I don't have cookies for all of you, too."

"That's okay," Bruno Ugg said.

"The dog and the chicken seem to like you," I said.

"Well, I like them," the little old lady said. "They always know."

"We are looking for sidewalk drawings," Loretta Fischetti said. "Do you know if there are any in the park?"

"There is one up the path," the little old lady said, indicating one of the walks that crisscross Tesev Noskecnil Park. "I hope you enjoy it."

We started up the path, and the little old lady went off in the direction of Hudson Street. We saw her climbing the steps of one of the old houses as we came upon the picture.

"I don't believe it!" Loretta Fischetti said. "It's a Vincent!"

"It is!" Bruno Ugg said. "And it's sunflowers! We were just talking about them."

It was a Vincent, there wasn't any doubt. The wild way the sunflowers were painted was like Vincent. Besides, there was his name, right across the middle of the yellow and gray vase the sunflowers were in: Vincent (LC).

"This picture is good," I said.

"It is," Loretta Fischetti said.

"I like the way he did that line around the vase," Bruno Ugg said.

"And look how the sunflowers are all different," Loretta Fischetti said.

"Do you think he painted the blue background first, or did the sunflowers and vase and then painted the background?" I asked.

"It's some good picture," Bruno Ugg said. "I think he had a real vase of sunflowers there, while he was painting."

"He must have. These are real flowers—he didn't do it from memory or anything."

"So the flowers in this picture really existed, a hundred years ago, or whenever it was, and they are gone, but they still exist in the painting," Loretta Fischetti said.

"And this is a copy of the painting," I said. "So they exist at least twice. Sort of neat."

"I wonder what the *LC* after his name means," Bruno Ugg said.

XVII

"**L**ucy Casserole," a voice behind us said. It was Meehan the Bum, sitting on a park bench. Meehan the Bum is a friend of ours. He gets around about as much as Jolly Roger, only with less dignity. Meehan the Bum is crazy, but he knows a lot.

"Lucy Casserole?"

"Yes," Meehan the Bum said. "Since the drawing is a copy of a painting by Vincent Van Gogh (which painting is in the Philadelphia Museum of Art, by the way), and since the Vincent signature is in the actual painting, as opposed to down in the corner, the screever, Lucy Casserole, added her initials after the name Vincent to indicate that she was the copyist."

"You know a lot about art?" Loretta

Fischetti asked Meehan the Bum.

"I almost graduated from the Hoboken Academy of Beaux Arts," Meehan the Bum said, jerking his thumb at the building at the edge of the park, which had been an art school but was now just an office building. "I would have graduated, but the Democrats had me thrown out for uttering insane remarks during lectures."

You have to know how to listen to Meehan the Bum. He makes sense for a while, and then he veers off into ranting about the Democrats.

"You went to art school?" I asked Meehan the Bum.

"Yes. At least I'm fairly sure I did. Art school, or barber college . . . or maybe it was law school. Anyway, they spoiled it for me."

"The Democrats?"

"They're antibum. That's why I hate them," Meehan the Bum said.

"You said screever," Loretta Fischetti said.

"I deny it," Meehan the Bum said. "Sometimes the Democrats make me say odd things. They do it with lasers. That's how

they got me thrown out of art school."

"A screever is a sidewalk artist, right?" Bruno Ugg asked.

"Right," Meehan the Bum said.

"And Lucy Casserole is a famous screever?" Loretta Fischetti asked.

"Right. Famous screever," Meehan the Bum said.

"And do you know her?" I asked.

"You know her yourself," Meehan the Bum said. "You were just talking to her."

"The little old lady?"

"Lucy Casserole," Meehan the Bum said. "She specializes in French Impressionists, but she does some good classical European paintings, and animal subjects."

"The little old lady who was just here?"

"I suspect her of being a Democrat," Meehan the Bum said. "But she's one of the good ones."

"She did this drawing of sunflowers by Van Gogh?"

"Yep. I saw her do it," Meehan the Bum said. "Nice little old lady."

Meehan the Bum lurched off, mumbling about how it was the Democrats' fault that there are no more good bagels. Jolly Roger trotted after him, not so much to keep Meehan the Bum company, it seemed to me, but because he was curious about where he was going and what he might do.

The three of us kids and Henrietta looked at the copy of the Van Gogh sunflowers.

"Lucy Casserole," Bruno Ugg said.

"The famous screever," I said.

"She sure is a good artist," Loretta Fischetti said.

"I wish I could draw this well," Bruno Ugg said.

"Do you suppose Lucy Casserole would

give us some pointers?" I asked.

"She seemed friendly," Loretta Fischetti said.

"We could ask her the next time we see her around," I said.

"Or we could ring her doorbell," Loretta Fischetti said.

"Could we just do that?" Bruno Ugg asked.

"I don't see why not," Loretta Fischetti said. "We'll be nice and polite. We'll apologize for bothering her, and ask if she has some time to talk to us—and tell her we will go away if she's busy."

"I can't imagine she'd object, if we are polite and say all that," I said.

"Maybe we could bring her a present," Bruno Ugg said. "Maybe a meat loaf sandwich."

"Not a meat loaf sandwich," Loretta Fischetti said.

"Doughnuts?" Bruno Ugg suggested.

"Flowers!" I said. "She's an artist, and she likes flowers. We can bring her sunflowers!"

"Where do we get them?" Bruno Ugg asked.

"I think I saw some growing in the empty lot on Willow Street," I said.

"It's a good idea," Loretta Fischetti said. "Let's go find the sunflowers, and then we'll ring Lucy Casserole's doorbell."

XIX

We got a nice bunch of sunflowers. They were in better shape than the ones in the Van Gogh picture, which were interesting but a little crummy.

"Maybe we ought to beat these up a little," Bruno Ugg said.

"No, I think when you give someone flowers they ought to be nice," Loretta Fischetti said. "Do you remember which house she went into?"

"I think it was this one," Bruno Ugg said.

We climbed up the stairs. There, next to one of the doorbells, was a little card with the name L. Casserole, neatly printed.

"So, push the button," Bruno Ugg said.

"You push it," I said.

"It doesn't matter who pushes it," Loretta Fischetti said.

"Then you push it," I said.

"I will," Loretta Fischetti said.

"Well, go ahead and push it," Bruno Ugg said.

"I'm going to," Loretta Fischetti said. "Hold up the sunflowers so she'll see them when she opens the door."

I held up the sunflowers.

Loretta Fischetti pushed the button.

We heard a loud buzz.

"What's that?" I asked.

"She's buzzing us in," Loretta Fischetti said. "Push the door open."

"Push the door open?"

"Haven't you ever rung a doorbell before?" Loretta Fischetti pushed the door open, and the buzzing stopped. "Now we go inside," she said.

We went inside, through a mostly glass door, and were in a hallway with a staircase.

"Come right up," we heard Lucy Casserole say.

We started up the stairs.

Lucy Casserole was standing in the doorway of her apartment.

"Oh, it's the nice children . . . and the chicken! Isn't the doggie with you?"

"No, Ms. Casserole," Bruno Ugg said. "He went off to follow Meehan the Bum."

Lucy Casserole made us tell her our names, and shook hands with each of us. Then she said, "Won't you come in? And are those wonderful sunflowers for me?" I stuck out my hand with the bunch of sunflowers.

"Such amazing things, sunflowers," Lucy Casserole said. "You know, each sunflower head consists of a thousand or more individual flowers. When they are in the bud stage, the plant follows the movement of the sun from east to west. Once the flower opens, it usually faces east. They are beautiful in the morning, glowing in the rays of the sun. And it is the state flower of Kansas. I will put them in a vase, and we can all draw them."

There was a long, narrow hallway leading

from the front door into Lucy Casserole's living room. It was a perfect little old lady living room, with all sorts of antique furniture, little pictures of roses in frames on the walls, an old-fashioned fireplace, and a big mirror.

Next to the living room was the dining room, but it wasn't exactly like a dining room. There was a sheet over the table, and on it were boxes of big, square, colored chalks and jars of paint. Against the walls were four big artist's easels, each with a big piece of extra-thick gray cardboard, and tacked to the cardboard were sheets of edible oatmeal paper.

Lucy Casserole tottered in with the sunflowers in a vase. It was a lot like the vase in the Van Gogh picture she had copied on the pavement.

"We can put the sunflowers here on the table," Lucy Casserole said. "And perhaps you children would like to work at these easels. Will the chicken be comfortable sitting on the sofa?"

"Do you give art lessons or something?" Bruno Ugg asked.

"Sometimes I do," Lucy Casserole said. "Today I will draw along with you, if you don't mind. Later we will have tea . . . and cookies."

XX

"What do we do, exactly," I asked.

"Do? You may do anything you like," Lucy Casserole said. "For myself, the first thing I am going to do is breathe."

"Breathe?"

"Yes, like this," Lucy Casserole said. She put her hands up in the air, with her fingers spread, and wiggled them.

"Like this?" we asked.

"Take deep breaths, children," Lucy Casserole said. "And stretch, stretch, stretch, as high as you can."

Lucy Casserole was wiggling her hands, stretching as high as she could—which was not very high—and bouncing up and down on her toes.

"Why are we doing this?" Loretta Fischetti asked.

"We are preparing to draw," Lucy Casserole said. "Now, perhaps you would like to put your arms out to the sides, and breathe, breathe, breathe."

We breathed, breathed, breathed. The fact was, it felt sort of nice. We found we were giggling a little.

"Now I am going to look at the sunflowers," Lucy Casserole said. "I will look right at them, and I will look at them out of the corner of my eye. I will look at them with my eyes wide open, and with my eyes half closed. I will try to look at just the colors, and I will try to look at just the shapes. Now I am looking at the light and shadows. You may want to look too, children."

We looked. As we looked, and as Lucy Casserole talked about different ways she was looking at the sunflowers, I started noticing things about them that I hadn't noticed before. The stems, for example—they were green and brown and strong—and . . .

I don't know . . . important.

"I'm looking at the vase, too," Lucy Casserole said. "It's an earthenware vase. I'm seeing how it's rough, and smooth, and round, and do you notice how it almost reflects the colors of the sunflowers? See how heavy it is."

It was a great vase.

"You will find these big chalks are very nice to use," Lucy Casserole said. "They are soft, and the colors are very rich. See how nicely the paper takes the chalk."

Lucy Casserole began to put some yellow on one of the sheets of paper, with little rapid strokes. Then she drew a long line with light green, and again with dark green, and then with light brown—and I saw a stalk.

Loretta Fischetti was already drawing. Soon Bruno Ugg and I were drawing too. The chalks were nice. They were soft and creamy, and I liked the way the color appeared on the paper.

We drew for a long time. The only sounds were the soft brushing sound of chalk on paper and breathing. Sometimes I would stop drawing and just look at the sunflowers—then I'd see something they were doing that I wanted to put in my picture.

Drawing on the big paper, standing in front of the easels, and after stretching our arms and breathing, we found we were drawing bigger. Before this, I would hold the pastel, or the crayon, or the brush as if it were a pencil, and work with my nose close to the paper and my wrist bent. Here, at Lucy Casserole's, I stood back from the paper and made bigger movements. My sunflowers filled up the whole big sheet of paper. I was amazed at how good my drawing looked.

"I think my drawing is finished," Loretta Fischetti said. "What do I do now?"

"Mine is finished too," Bruno Ugg said.

"Mine too," I said.

"This might be a good time to have tea," Lucy Casserole said. "Perhaps you children would like to carry your drawing boards into the living room and lean them against the étagère, while I get the tea."

We figured out that the étagère was the fancy piece of furniture at the end of the room. We dragged in the big sheets of heavy cardboard, with our drawings pinned on, and stood them on the floor, leaning against it.

In a little while, Lucy Casserole tottered in with a big tray, with a teapot and cups and spoons and such. She put the tray on a little

78

table, and settled into a chair behind it.

"Now, children, you may come get your tea, and find places to sit. Then we can look at our pictures," Lucy Casserole said. "Mr. Ugg, will you please place that lamp on the floor, and switch it on—we want some light on the drawings." It was one of those gooseneck desk lamps. Bruno Ugg pointed it at the drawings and turned it on.

Lucy Casserole asked each of us whether we wanted milk and sugar in our tea—we all said yes. She poured out a little saucer of milk for Henrietta. She also handed cookies around. Henrietta had two.

Henrietta seemed to be having a particularly good time. She sat on the sofa, sipping her milk and nibbling her cookies delicately.

"Henrietta seems quite at home here," I said.

"Oh, Henrietta has been my guest many times," Lucy Casserole said. "I find her a very polite and pleasant chicken."

"She's been here before?" I asked.

"Many times," Lucy Casserole said. "But not of late."

There had been that period, before Vic Trola gave Henrietta to me to look after, when she had been going off on her own at night. Apparently one of the things she did was visit Lucy Casserole.

"Now, if you like, we can look at the pictures," Lucy Casserole said. "See how each of you has your very own way of seeing, and drawing, the sunflowers."

First I noticed that we had all done great drawings—but, as Lucy Casserole had suggested, they were all different. Mine was all about color—I really liked it. It looked like fireworks. I had taken to using the flat sides of the chalks, and I put in touches of bright red and orange that weren't really so bright in the real flowers.

Loretta Fischetti's drawing had more browns and dark greens in it. It was quieter than mine, and looked more like the actual sunflowers.

Bruno Ugg had used thick black lines for the stems, and to outline the sunflowers and the vase. It looked like a stained-glass window.

Lucy Casserole's picture looked like Vincent Van Gogh had done it.

Lucy Casserole pointed out things about the pictures, and asked us questions about why we had done things the way we did, and what we thought about the pictures—but mostly we sat quietly, sipped our tea, and looked.

"Will you be our art teacher?" Bruno Ugg asked.

"Yes, please give us more drawing lessons," Loretta Fischetti said.

"I would enjoy that very much," Lucy Casserole said. "But I'm afraid I would have to charge you. The chalks, you know—they're quite expensive."

"We understand," I said. "We would want to pay, of course—if it's not too expensive."

"I could see the three of you—and of course, you may bring Henrietta—once a week . . . and my fee would be one dollar and twenty-five cents each—no charge for the chicken," Lucy Casserole said.

"So, do you know a lot about art?" I asked my father.

"I took two semesters of art appreciation, old fig," my father said.

Old fig is one of the things my father calls me. He also calls me old man, old bean, old shoe, old walrus. This is all part of his talking like an Englishman in the movies, although he was born in Jersey City, New Jersey, and has never even seen England.

"Does having taken two semesters of art appreciation mean you know a lot about art?" I asked.

"It means I know a bit, old kangaroo," my father said. "What in particular were you interested in?"

"Well, if a person wanted to learn about art, what would you suggest that person do?" I asked.

"That person should visit the Metropolitan Museum of Art," my father said. "They have scads of art there. Oodles of art, in fact. Pictures by the hundreds and thousands, also statuary, textiles, arms and armor, chunks of ancient Egyptian temples, watercolors, oil paintings, medieval tapestries, pottery, huge urns made of semiprecious stones, Chinese Foo dogs, ancient Roman sarcoghagi, and a suit of clothes worn by Alexander Hamilton. That's where one goes to learn about art."

"It's in New York City, isn't it?" I asked.

"Right on Fifth Avenue, old sport," my father said.

"Can we go there?"

"We can."

"When?"

"Well, just now your mother and I are prying all the molding off the doorframes. Then we plan to do a lot of sandpapering and scraping and varnishing. So we can't go with you anytime soon. Why don't you just go yourself?"

"Am I allowed to go into Manhattan by myself?" I asked my father.

"Aren't you?" my father asked. "Let me check with the memsa'b."

Memsa'b is one of the things he calls my mother.

"Sweetyboots!" my father called. "Is the young chap allowed to go to Manhattan on his own?"

Sweetyboots is another name he calls my mother. She was on top of a ladder, unscrewing a light fixture on the third floor. "Why does he want to go?" she called down to my father.

"Wants to visit the museum," my father called up to her.

"That's the kind of cultural resource we didn't have in the suburbs!" my mother shouted. "I am so pleased that our son wants to visit a museum."

"It seems you are allowed," my father said.

84

"I was thinking of going with my friends," I said.

"The young blighter wants to go with his friends," my father called up to my mother.

"With his urban friends who are interested in culture!" my mother called down. "I don't care if it takes us ten years to fix up this old house—we did the right thing bringing our child to grow up in a stimulating environment."

I thought ten years was a fairly optimistic guess. It's more likely that my parents will still be trying to get the house in shape when I am seventy-five years old.

"Just one thing, old bat," my father said.

"Yes?" I asked.

"If you do go into the city, take the chicken."

"Henrietta?"

"Yes, old pickle. No harm will come to you with the bloomin' chicken by your side. Promise you'll take her."

"But the museum . . . ," I said. "Will they let a chicken, even a six-foot-tall one, into the museum?"

"That's a good point, old bagel," my father said. "It's quite likely the museum doesn't allow animals. But there's a simple solution—if she can't be admitted as a chicken, we will simply disguise her as something else."

"Disguise her?"

"It's an innocent deception," my father said. "When the museum wallahs made the rules, they couldn't have been thinking of well-behaved giant chickens. We will simply dress her up as something else."

"What?" I asked. "I mean, she's a chicken, a very tall, heavyset chicken. What disguise would get her into a museum?"

"It so happens I have the very thing," my father said.

"You do?"

"Do you remember my Halloween costume from two years ago?" my father asked. "I still have it."

"The nun's habit?" I asked.

"Spot on, old beanbag," my father said. "I think it will fit Henrietta perfectly."

"I have to think about this," I said.

"It's a wizard idea," my father said. "And I absolutely forbid you to go to the city without Henrietta to protect you. I should say, Sister Henrietta."

XXIII

"**W**e're really not supposed to go to the city without an adult," Loretta Fischetti said.

"We went to Davis Davisdavis's," I said.

"True, but we just zipped in, got our art supplies, and zipped back," Loretta Fischetti said. "It was just doing an errand. Going way uptown to the museum is sort of different."

"And probably we'd want to look around and get something to eat," Bruno Ugg said.

"Henrietta is adult," I said.

"She's an adult chicken," Loretta Fischetti said.

"She'll be dressed as a nun," I said.

"I don't see how that makes a big difference," Loretta Fischetti said.

"Maybe we could buy hot dogs from

one of those wagons they have," Bruno Ugg said.

We were in the basement, drawing pictures of a vase with some weeds in it, a bowl of tennis balls, and part of a tricycle we had found in my basement next door. We had arranged all the stuff on top of an orange crate.

Loretta Fischetti's mother came down with a load of laundry and some oatmeal cookies for us.

"Nick, your mother says you children are planning to go to the museum," Loretta Fischetti's mother said. "You all have to promise to stay together, and Henrietta must be with you at all times."

"So it's all right for me to go?" Loretta Fischetti asked her mother.

"I suppose so," Loretta Fischetti's mother said. "I can't see anything wrong with children visiting a museum with a nun."

"She's a chicken."

"Nick's father says she knows hen-fu," Loretta Fischetti's mother said. "So, I imagine you'll be perfectly safe. And your mother agrees, Bruno. She would like you to bring her a postcard from the museum shop—something by Salvador Dali."

"They have a shop? Cool!" Bruno Ugg said.

XXIV

We were having our first official art lesson at Lucy Casserole's. We were all arranged in front of our drawing boards. Henrietta, too— she was playing with some pieces of colored chalk, and Lucy Casserole had given her a bowl of broken gingersnaps to nibble.

"Now, children," Lucy Casserole said. "After we do our breathing and stretching, I want to tell you about an experiment you may enjoy. Perhaps you would like to hear about it."

We said we would.

"Good. I am sure you will like it," Lucy Casserole said. "Now, be sure to stand on tiptoe, and reach as high as you can. Wiggle your fingers and try to touch the ceiling, and stretch, stretch, stretch. Don't forget to breathe, children."

We stretched, and wiggled our fingers, and breathed. Henrietta stretched her wings up and did a little dance, turning around in place.

"Yes, yes, we are getting oxygen into our lungs, and then into our bloodstreams—and our blood carries the oxygen to our brains. The brain must have oxygen, children." Lucy Casserole was stretching and wiggling and breathing with us.

"What is the experiment you were talking about?" Loretta Fischetti asked Lucy Casserole.

"You may all try it, if you like," Lucy Casserole said. Then she stopped speaking, and just waited until we all said we would like to try it. I had noticed that Lucy Casserole never directly asked us to do anything, and she never asked questions that could be answered with a yes or a no. She would just say we could do this or that, if we wanted to. Then we would have to decide if we wanted to do whatever it was and tell her. I sort of liked Lucy Casserole's way of talking to us—

it suggested that she thought we had minds of our own.

"The first thing is to make a scribble with our eyes closed," Lucy Casserole said.

"Make a scribble?" Bruno Ugg asked.

"See? I am standing before my easel," Lucy Casserole said. "I place one hand on the upper corner of the drawing board, and I have a piece of chalk in my other hand. Now, I close my eyes, and scrible, scribble, scribble, right in the middle of the paper, and going just anywhere."

"That's the experiment?" I asked.

"That's the first part of the experiment," Lucy Casserole said. "Perhaps you'd all like to make your scribbles now. Remember to keep your eyes closed."

We scribbled. It felt sort of silly—like something little kids in nursery school would do.

"What's the second part of the experiment?" Loretta Fischetti asked when we had finished scribbling.

"Have you ever looked at clouds, and imagined they resembled things—whales, for example, or ships?"

We looked at one another.

"Or have you ever looked at the patterns in cloth or wallpaper, and seen pictures?" Lucy Casserole asked.

"I looked at leaves in the park once, and saw faces," Bruno Ugg said.

"That looking at a random arrangement of clouds, or wallpaper, or leaves, is how our experiment works," Lucy Casserole said. "We can look at our scribbles—sometimes it helps to squint a little—and the first image we see we have to draw—that is the rule."

"Draw it on the same sheet of paper?" I asked.

"Yes," Lucy Casserole said. "If you see a whale, draw the whale. And if you see more whales, you can draw them, too. And, of course, you can add things you didn't see the first time you squinted—make as complete a drawing as you can."

We were already squinting.

"I will do the exercise along with you," Lucy Casserole said. "Just to get you started. I am looking, looking, looking at my scribble, not in a hurry, just waiting until I see something, my eyes half closed, breathing quietly."

"I see something!" Bruno Ugg said. "But I don't know what it is."

"Perhaps if you start to draw it, it will turn into something you recognize," Lucy Casserole said.

Bruno Ugg was drawing. "It's a wheel," he said. "And this is water. It's like a waterwheel . . . no! It's a paddle wheel. And these are smokestacks!"

Life on the Mississippi, by Mark Twain, was practically Bruno Ugg's favorite Classics Comic. He was drawing one of those Mississippi paddle-wheel steamboats.

"Mine is a bird!" Loretta Fischetti said. "It's a big bird in flight—like an eagle! And there are mountains! And this is a river."

Mine was a house. It was an old house, like the one I lived in. It *was* the one I lived in. And there was a bicycle—my bicycle. My bike had been stolen the very first day we lived in Hoboken, but I got it back. And riding my bicycle was Henrietta, who actually can ride one, something few chickens can do.

We drew and drew, adding details to our pictures. Lucy Casserole was drawing too, and Henrietta made some marks on her paper, holding pieces of chalk in her beak. She also ate some bits of broken gingersnaps, and she ate some chalk.

After a while, our pictures were finished, and we stood back and looked at them. It was surprising what complicated pictures we had made, starting with random scribbles. Bruno Ugg had done a whole Mississippi River scene, the steamboat with smoke pouring out, and trees and fields, and blue water.

Loretta Fischetti's big bird was soaring over mountains, and my house and bicycle looked good.

Lucy Casserole had done a picture of an old lady in a black dress, with a white lace cap, sitting in a chair with her hands in her lap, and her feet on a little footstool—all in gray and black.

Next came the sitting around, sipping tea, and looking at our pictures.

"This is very good work," Lucy Casserole said. "Does anyone want to say anything about his or her picture?"

"I was surprised," Loretta Fischetti said. "I don't know where that bird came from."

"Where do you think it might have come from?" Lucy Casserole asked.

"I guess it was there, in my imagination," Loretta Fischetti said.

"Isn't it interesting what things are there, in our imaginations?" Lucy Casserole said.

"Your picture looks sort of familiar," I said to Lucy Casserole. "It's like I've seen it before."

"It's by James McNeill Whistler," Lucy Casserole said. *Portrait of the Artist's Mother*, painted in 1871. The original is in the Musée d'Orsay in Paris."

"You painted someone else's picture?" Bruno Ugg asked. "It was in your imagination?"

"Well, that comes from being a screever for so many years," Lucy Casserole said. "I have drawn so many famous pictures on sidewalks—hundreds of them—I just have them in my head. It's as though I carry a whole art museum around with me."

"We are planning to go to an art museum," I said.

"Yes?" Lucy Casserole asked.

"Yes," I said. "We plan to visit the Metropolitan Museum of Art in New York City."

"And it will be your first visit to an art museum?" Lucy Casserole asked.

"Yes, our very first."

"I am not sure that is a very good idea," Lucy Casserole said.

"You're not? Why not?" I asked.

"It's too big," Lucy Casserole said.

"We will have an adult with us," I said.

"When I say it's too big, I mean there is a lot to take in all at once—when it's your very first time. I have a lot of experience with children and museums. You see, I did a great deal of screeving in that part of town—and I used to be a noony."

"A noony?"

"Yes. Many children who live on the Upper East Side have nannies. You know what a nanny is?"

"Like Mary Poppins?"

"That's right. A nanny looks after children."

"And what's a noony?" we asked Lucy Casserole.

"A noony fills in for a nanny at lunchtime, and looks after the children while the nanny takes a break. I would screeve in the mornings and afternoons, and in the middle of the day I would noony. So, I took many children to the museums—and the Metropolitan is a tall order."

"In what way is it a tall order?" we asked.

"First you find yourself in the biggest, highest room you have ever seen. It is next to impossible not to try out the echo. Sometimes there are a hundred children trying out the echo. Some of them feel the need to run. And there are big doorways and a staircase leading to galleries with so many things, and people going everywhere, looking at things—and so many things to look at. It can be overwhelming. It's hard to settle down and look at things properly."

"We wouldn't try out the echo," Bruno Ugg said.

"Or run," Loretta Fischetti said.

"I'm sure you wouldn't," Lucy Casserole said. "But for a first visit, a smaller museum, with just the right things in it, might be a better choice."

"Do you have such a museum in mind?" I asked.

"I have," Lucy Casserole said.

XXVI

"So, old Fig Newton," my father said. "Is everything shipshape and Bristol fashion?"

"You mean, is everything properly organized?" I asked him.

"Yes, for your trip to the good old museum," my father said. "Is everything tickety-boo?"

"Well, we know what bus to take in Manhattan, and we know where to get off, and we know how to get back to the tubes. We know where it is, when it opens, how much it costs to get in, and that children under sixteen must be accompanied by an adult."

"Which you will be," my father said.

"Yes, an adult chicken."

"Tickety-boo," my father said. "And you have decided to visit the Frick Collection instead of the Metropolitan."

"We have," I said. "It was Lucy Casserole's suggestion. She feels that the larger museum might be too much for us, the first time. The Frick Collection only has about a hundred and fifty pictures, but Lucy Casserole says every one is a lollapalooza."

"Now, this Lucy Casserole," my father said. "She is a qualified art teacher?"

"She's a retired screever," I said.

"Oh! Well! You can't beat a screever," my father said.

"She even said we shouldn't try to look at all the pictures," I said. "She said we should just glance around in general, and then pick one of the rooms, and only really spend time with maybe four or five pictures. She said that is the way to look at things in a museum. If you try to take everything in, you won't really remember anything vividly."

"Seems to me there must be blokes who

can look at more than four or five pictures," my father said.

"I think that comes with practice," I said. "Anyway, Lucy Casserole told us to just sample things, and only spend time with a few pictures, and not make ourselves tired."

"Blimey! There must be more to looking at pictures than I thought," my father said. "Now, if you should get lost, what will you do?"

"Ask a policeman," I said.

"Or follow the chicken," my father said. "And if strange, evil-looking, or rough people approach you?"

"Find a policeman?"

"Or let the chicken deal with it. And will you buy hot dogs from those carts in the street?"

"No," I said. "Because you have explained to me that they are factories for bacteria. We will buy sesame-seed bagels and large pickles from a reputable-looking delicatessen."

"Only a suggestion, old top," my father said. "But it is the very best New York City street lunch, in my humble opinion. Also a cream soda goes very well."

"Now I have to ask you a question," I said. "Have you tried the nun costume on Henrietta?"

"Wait until you see her," my father said.

XXVII

It went without a hitch. As far as we could tell, no one paid the least attention to Henrietta, and no one seemed to notice that she was a chicken. Henrietta appeared to like wearing the nun costume, and she seemed quite happy riding the train and the bus.

"It just occurred to me," Bruno Ugg said. "Do you suppose it's against the law to impersonate a nun?"

"It's not an official nun's habit," Loretta Fischetti said. "It's just a costume from a costume store."

"How would that make any difference?" Bruno Ugg said.

"Well, she can't be accused of stealing it from an actual nun," Loretta Fischetti said.

"That's one thing. Besides, I sincerely doubt there is a law on the books that says a chicken can't wear a costume. How often do you suppose such a thing comes up?"

"Our stop is coming up," I said. "Let's get ready to get off the bus."

We had to walk a block over to Fifth Avenue. I must say, we looked completely normal—three kids and a nun walking along the street.

We were impressed when we got to the Frick Collection. Lucy Casserole had told us that it was Mr. Frick's house—where he lived—before he left it to be a museum. It was some house. Right away, we saw that she had been right about the Metropolitan Museum being too big for our first time. The Frick Collection looked plenty big enough.

"Okay, look normal going in," Bruno Ugg said. "Just act like we come to places like this all the time."

There was a guard, wearing a uniform, at the entrance. We were shaking in our shoes. He was looking right at Henrietta. If he spotted her as a chicken, we'd be thrown out for certain.

"Sister Wendy!" the guard said. "What an honor to have you visit our museum! Do come right in!"

We had money in our hands, to pay our admission, but the guard just waved us through.

"There will be no charge for you and your young friends, Sister Wendy," the guard said. "We hope you enjoy your visit."

Henrietta bobbed her head up and down a couple of times.

"He thinks he knows her," Loretta Fischetti whispered.

"Who's Sister Wendy?" I whispered.

"I think that's the art nun on TV," Bruno Ugg whispered. "She goes around to museums and gives talks about the art."

We clustered around Henrietta as she whisked past the guard and into a big open space with a fountain and statues. She stopped for a moment, turned left, turned right, and then took off fast. We had to hurry

to keep up with her. I was afraid she might start clucking, or running. Suddenly she veered left—and left again. We were hanging onto her costume.

This was scary. We hadn't counted on an out-of-control chicken in the museum. Where was she going so fast? What was going on? Big paintings flashed past us as we rushed up one side of a huge long room and down the other. There was no time to look at anything as we scurried to keep up with the bustling nun-chicken.

She came to a stop in a smaller room than the big gallery we had just flashed through. Henrietta was standing in front of a painting. She was looking at it. We looked at it too. It was the most fantastic thing I had ever seen in my life.

It showed a guy wearing a monk's robe. He was standing on these greenish rocks, outside a sort of cave that had been fixed up with a little gate—and there was a little table, knocked together out of some pieces of wood, with a book and a skull on it. In the background there were cultivated fields, and there were hills and mountains, and a castle, and a sky that looked like Vincent might have painted it, if Vincent had been sane. And there was this little tree, up in the left-hand corner—just an ordinary little tree—in fact, everything in the picture was sort of ordinary, only . . . only . . .

Well, the thing about this picture was . . . you could tell that everything was so very important. It was magical. There was this light in the picture. It was soft, but powerful. It wasn't regular light. It was . . .

"Wow," I said.

"Wow," Loretta Fischetti said.

"Wow," Bruno Ugg said.

"Wow, wow, wow."

"It says it's St. Francis," Bruno Ugg said, reading the little card.

"Was he the one who liked animals?" I asked.

"Look, there's a donkey, and some kind of bird," Loretta Fischetti said. "And those are sheep in the distance."

"A guy named Giovanni Bellini painted

this," Bruno Ugg said. "And, get this—he painted it in the year fourteen eighty."

"That's more than five hundred years ago!"

"Is that possible? It looks brand-new!"

"Kiddies, this picture is so brand-new that it's the newest thing in town. It was brand-new when he did it in fourteen eighty, and it is brand-new this minute. It's so brand-new that most people haven't evolved to the point where they can understand it yet."

Someone else was speaking. It was an unshaven old guy in rumpled pants and a rumpled coat, wearing a rumpled hat.

"One of the things I like about this picture is how smart it is," the old guy said. "Everything in it means something—old St. Francis's sandals under his desk, the little water spout down there in the corner, that little jug, the hunk of rope hanging off the trellis, so you can ring the saint's doorbell—all those things have what we call symbolic meaning. But that was just Bellini having extra fun. Look how he signed his name! See the little scrap of paper that's blown up against those twigs? There's where he put his handle. Oh, he knew he had brought off a world-beating masterpiece, and he just put in some extra touches, because he was feeling so good. But the light! Look at the light, kiddies! And those rocks! You feel that you can reach out and touch them. And there's old Francis, knowing for sure that he's got the message—just the way Bellini felt when he put the last brushstrokes on this lollapalooza."

"Lucy Casserole said this museum had lollapaloozas," I said.

The rumpled old guy was standing next to the painting, beaming up at it, looking as proud as though he had painted it himself. "Lucy Casserole? You know Lucy Casserole?"

"She's our art teacher," Loretta Fischetti said.

"She's a fun girl," the old rumpled guy said. "Quite the screever. Tell her you met me. My name is Hilangully Ryder."

"Hilangully?"

"Ryder. Albert Pinkham Ryder was my grandpa. He was a painter. So am I."

This whole time we had not been able to

take our eyes off the painting of St. Francis in the desert. We had only glimpsed Hilangully Ryder out of the corners of our eyes. Having a conversation at the same time as being inside the world of the painting felt weird and dreamlike.

"Since you are pupils of Lucy Casserole, I am sure she would approve of what I am going to tell you next," Hilangully Ryder said. "Do just as I say. Turn around, fast. Now!"

We did it. We spun around.

"Yipes!"

"Yike!"

"Eeek!"

"Meet another saint, kiddies," Hilangully Ryder said. "This is St. Jerome, painted about a hundred years later by Domenikos Theotokopoulos, better known as El Greco, which means 'The Greek.' Quite a contrast, isn't it?"

We were breathing hard.

Where the St. Francis was amazing and beautiful and full of details and drew you in, St. Jerome was simple and full of fire and jumped out at you. It was this skinny old guy with white hair and a white beard, wearing a red robe, with his hands on a Bible—and he had a look in his eyes that made you feel like he was about to say something astonishing. After looking at the other picture, it was as though someone had rung a bell—a loud bell.

"That's a lollapalooza too, isn't it?" Bruno Ugg said.

"El Greco specialized in lollapaloozas," Hilangully Ryder said. "Look what he did with those cardinal's robes. And look at that right hand. It's like a monument fifty feet high. When you come upon it suddenly, it couldn't be more surprising than if you found yourself looking at a wild bull elephant. By the way, that's a nice chicken."

"Hey, take it easy," Loretta Fischetti said. "She's the adult we're here with."

"Okay, kids. I got it. Shtoom's the word." Hilangully Ryder put his finger to his lips. "Interesting what people who don't know how to look at things don't see. Now, come over here—in this very same room is the finest sleeve ever painted. The rest of the picture is pretty good, too."

The sleeve was on Sir Thomas More in a painting by Hans Holbein the Younger, painted in 1527. It was a velvet sleeve, and he had a lot of other fancy clothes and doodads. He was a smart-looking guy. I recognized the drapery behind him from the first sidewalk painting we saw by Lucy Casserole—the one of Henrietta.

"You children are looking a little glassy eyed," Hilangully Ryder said.

"It's our first time in an art museum," Loretta Fischetti said.

"Ah, I see," Hilangully Ryder said. "Maybe you should just stroll around for a short while—don't get too involved with the paintings—just look them over lightly. Then go out in the fresh air."

We said we thought that was a good idea.

Hilangully Ryder made us tell him our names, and told us to tell Lucy Casserole he would come to visit her soon.

Hilangully Ryder scurried off somewhere

and left us on our own. We staggered around the museum and saw some paintings that were amazing. We saw Rembrandts. We saw another El Greco.

"My brain is full," Bruno Ugg said.

"Mine, too," Loretta Fischetti said. "We have to come back here. But let's go now."

There was one more surprise for us. When we went outside in the street, everything looked different. Colors were different. Light was different. Everything we saw looked different—different from the way we saw it before we went inside the museum—and we knew it would never be the same.

XXVIII

"**S**he's back!" Loretta Fischetti burst into the basement, where Bruno Ugg and I were painting portraits of each other.

"Who's back?" Bruno Ugg and I asked Loretta Fischetti.

"Starr Lackawanna is back," Loretta Fischetti said. "And the library is open!"

"Let's go!"

"Hi, Starr Lackawanna," we all said at once. "How was your vacation on Baffin Island? Did you have fun kayaking? Did you see any polar bears? Do you have any art books? We want to check out art books. Do you have any books about famous painters? Do you have any books about Vincent Van Gogh? Do you have any books about Giovanni Bellini? Did you ever hear of a painter called Albert Pinkham Ryder? Do you have any books about how to draw? Will you take us to the Frick Collection sometime? We'll pay your bus fare and museum admission, and buy you a bagel and a pickle. We don't know how long they'll buy that Henrietta is Sister Wendy. Do you have any books about how to paint? What is Impressionism? How old do we have to be to go to art school? Who was better, Picasso or Rembrandt? What is chiaroscuro, and how do you pronounce it?"

"It's rough being without a librarian for a whole month, isn't it?" Starr Lackawanna said.

"Yes!" we all said.

"Well, your librarian is back, and I will be happy to help you find books and materials useful in the art mania you seem to have developed while I was away. First, I brought you all postcards."

Starr Lackawanna gave us three postcards. One showed incredible lights in the sky.

"Look at the colors!" Loretta Fischetti said.

"Those are the northern lights, or aurora borealis," Starr Lackawanna said.

"Do they really look like that?" I asked.

"I saw them," Starr Lackawanna said. "And this postcard is of a polar bear. I saw one of those, too. And this is an inukshuk—the Inuit people make these sculptures by piling stones on top of one another. You see, it is the figure of a person. They make them as markers so you can find your way home—and also because they look so neat."

"Cool!" Bruno Ugg said.

"Cool!" I said.

"I want to do a painting of these northern lights," Loretta Fischetti said.

"I'm going to paint the polar bear," I said.

"Now, art books," Starr Lackawanna said. "I have something that might be very good. It's called *Fun with Collage for Kids.*"

"A children's art book?"

"That's right," Starr Lackawanna said.

"We don't want any children's art books," I said. "We want to be real artists."

"Hold your horses," Starr Lackawanna said.

"Children can be real artists. In fact, children tend to be the realest artists. You don't want to get all professional and boring, do you? And, do you happen to know what collage, pronounced kol-ADJE, is?"

We didn't.

"Collage is a way of making pictures by cutting or tearing bits of paper and gluing them down. And you can use things you find, like pieces of the newspaper and pictures out of magazines. You can also use bits of cloth, grass, old Henrietta feathers, chewing-gum wrappers. Here is the book. What do you think?"

"Ohhh, this is neat," Bruno Ugg said.

"And look! You can paint on them too!" Loretta Fischetti said.

"I want to try this," I said.

"Not too childish?" Starr Lackawanna asked.

"No, this is good."

"And you will notice that some 'real' artists, like Matisse and Picasso, did collage," Starr Lackawanna said. "And the materials are mostly free."

"We're checking this book out," I said.

"Good choice," Starr Lackawanna said. "I will look for some other books and materials for you."

"We are going now," we told Starr Lackawanna. "We want to read this and make some collages. We're glad you are back."

"I am glad to be back," Starr Lackawanna said.

XXIX

The collage-making went well. We got plenty of glue, paste, and mucilage at Sean Vergessen's store and set right to work, snipping and cutting and tearing and gluing. There were tons of moldy old magazines in my basement. Some of the paper was yellowy and had little brown spots, which were interesting.

Bruno Ugg was very good at cutting images out of the magazines and putting them together to make weird pictures, like an airplane landing on a ham sandwich, or a ladies' girdle on the Empire State Building. Loretta Fischetti went in for abstract patterns of type from newspapers, going in all directions—and she added colors in tempera paint. My specialty was gluing down hunks of hair from nasty old dolls I found in the basement, also leaves, gum wrappers, and things like buttons, Popsicle sticks, and various pieces of trash. Bruno Ugg's mother came down with a load of laundry and suggested we use uncooked noodles and various shapes of pasta, which worked very well.

When it was time for our next art lesson, we took a bunch of collages along to show Lucy Casserole. She liked them a lot.

"Children, it is such a beautiful day," Lucy Casserole said. "I wonder if you might enjoy working outdoors. I was thinking, perhaps we could go to the park and draw from nature today."

We helped Lucy Casserole load paints, chalks, brushes, and rags into a little wagon, and with drawing pads under our arms, we dragged everything across the street to Tesev Noskecnil Park.

It *was* a beautiful day, and the park was nice, with trees and paths and the tall buildings of Manhattan across the river. We set everything up under a big tree. It was a little like a picnic, only we were painting instead of eating. Henrietta was nearby, swinging on the swings.

"I am going to just sit for a while," Lucy Casserole said. "I will first take in the whole scene before me. Then I will think about the light. I will notice where the shadows fall, and I will notice that leaves have a darker side and a lighter side, and as they move in the breeze, they seem to shimmer. Now I am looking at color. How many colors are the leaves? Are they just green, or are there blues and yellows and flashes of white? Are there colors in the shadows? Now I am looking at shapes. See how the trees are put together. See that the spaces between the trees are also shapes."

We sat and looked with Lucy Casserole. The more we looked, the more we saw that there was much more to see in Tesev Noskecnil Park than we had ever noticed before.

One by one, we stood up and did our breathing and stretching and finger wiggling. Then we settled down and began to draw. It was hard to get it right. My eyes went back and forth from the couple of trees I was trying to draw to my paper, and back again. I liked the bumps and angles in the tree trunks and branches. Loretta Fischetti was painting leaves in lots of different colors, and Bruno Ugg was trying to draw the whole park, using the colored chalks sideways and making big sweeping strokes. Lucy Casserole was doing a picture of some trees, and instead of Manhattan in the background, she had drawn Mount Fujiyama, which I recognized from a picture I had seen in *National Geographic*.

Meehan the Bum jumped on a bench and began striking muscle-man poses. "For a small fee, I could pose in the altogether," he said. "I am unashamed of nudeness and regard my body as a temple."

"Please, please, remain covered," Lucy Casserole said. "Your garments are so colorful."

"Should we try to draw him?" I asked.

"If you like," Lucy Casserole said. "But don't encourage him to disrobe. The police have spoken to him about that several times, and he is not to do it anymore."

Two figures appeared in the park. One was carrying a large cardboard carton, and the other had two shopping bags.

"As I live and breathe," Lucy Casserole said.

"It's Hilangully Ryder and Davis Davisdavis!"

It was the scruffy, rumpled guy we had met at the Frick Collection and the art supplies dealer, who was fairly scruffy and rumpled himself.

"Lucy Casserole! My finest customer!" Davis Davisdavis said. "And the three children wearing official Davis Davisdavis artists' berets! And an enormous chicken!"

"Hello, Lucy. How's it going, kids?" Hilangully Ryder said. Then to Bruno Ugg he said, "Try a little red under here, and put a touch of orange next to it. Nice work."

"What are you doing in Hoboken?" Lucy Casserole asked the two scruffy, rumpled men.

"I am delivering this large box of highest-quality colored chalks, hand made by the hill men of Nepal," Davis Davisdavis said. "And Mr. Hilangully Ryder, another of my fine customers, came along for the ride and to have a small eggplant picnic. We have enough for everybody. Will you join us?"

"Does that include me?" Meehan the Bum asked.

Hilangully Ryder peered at Meehan the

Bum. "Is that Pierpont Meehan?" he asked. "Weren't you at the Hoboken Academy of Beaux Arts in the old days?"

"Class of fifty-nine, expelled," Meehan the Bum said, bowing.

"Oh, yes, I remember you," Hilangully Ryder said. "You used to utter threats against the government."

"Also the church," Meehan the Bum said.

"An eggplant picnic?" Bruno Ugg asked.

"I was raised in the health-food business," Davis Davisdavis said. "Davis Davisdavis is a scientific eater. Davis Davisdavis has discovered that the noble eggplant is the perfect food, and lives on eggplants exclusively—those, and Dr. Pedwee's Grape Soda. Every dish in our picnic is made of eggplant. We have broiled eggplant, boiled eggplant, pickled eggplant strips, eggplant chips, eggplant puree, deviled eggplant, and delicious eggplant cookies with chocolate chips. Put down your drawing boards, children, and help Davis Davisdavis unpack the lunch."

XXX

It all tasted like eggplant to me. Good, but like eggplant. We lounged on the grass, enjoying our eggplant picnic, and sipping Dr. Pedwee's Grape Soda. Henrietta liked the delicious eggplant cookies with chocolate chips.

While we ate, Hilangully Ryder looked at the pictures we had been doing. "You're on the right track, kiddies," he said. "You're using your eyes. People talk about sudden inspiration, and talent, and genius—but art is mostly about hard mental work. It's more about looking than doing. You have to look at things scientifically, take them apart and put them back together. You have to learn to feel things with your eyes. And then you try—try, mind you—to put it all together in some new way.

And you have to know when you succeed, and when you fail—and why. You have to use your loaf." Hilangully Ryder smacked his head with the heel of his hand. "In other words, you have to think."

"Davis Davisdavis agrees," Davis Davisdavis said. "And you have a fine teacher." He bowed to Lucy Casserole.

"Well, I believe it is a good idea to breathe, stretch, wiggle your fingers, and then just give it your best shot," Lucy Casserole said.

"I think you ought to form a club," Hilangully Ryder said. "You can call yourselves the Artsy Smartsy Club. Do not call yourselves the Finger Wigglers Club."

"I am curious," Lucy Casserole said to Davis Davisdavis. "You have brought a very large box of square lecturer's chalks, such as I used in my former career as a screever."

"You were one of the great screevers," Davis Davisdavis said. "It is too bad you retired."

"Oh, I do a bit of screeving," Lucy Casserole said. "I keep my hand in—but just locally, and for my own amusement. What I am curious about is for whom is that very large box of chalks? It appears to contain more than I could have used in a year of screeving."

"I am to deliver this box of chalks to the committee in charge of the First Annual Hoboken Street Art Festival and Competition," Davis Davisdavis said.

"That would be me," Meehan the Bum said.

"You?" we all asked.

"Yes," Meehan the Bum said. "The Hoboken Department of Recreation and Culture has asked me to organize a grand festival of street art. I suppose they chose me because of my long association with culture, my outgoing personality, and my organizational skills. Also, nobody else wanted to do it. The chalks will be provided free of charge to participants— and I was going to ask you, Ms. Casserole, if you would be one of the judges. The other judges will be the mayor and myself."

"I will be pleased to act as a judge," Lucy

Casserole said. "When does the event take place?"

"Saturday," Meehan the Bum said.

"How come we haven't heard about this?" I asked.

"You're hearing about it now," Meehan the Bum said. "You can register and pick up your chalks at the city hall at eight A.M. on the day."

"I will be a judge too," Hilangully Ryder said. "Also, I will be a participant. And Davis Davisdavis will be a judge."

"Sure. Why not?" Meehan the Bum said.

XXXI

The Artsy Smartsy Club held a meeting in the basement.

"We're going to enter the competition, right?"

"Of course."

"Shall we all work on one picture, or do separate ones?"

"We'll have a better chance if we split up."

"Shall we copy famous paintings, like Lucy Casserole does?"

"Or should we do our own original ones?"

"We should practice."

"Fortunately, we have chalks of our own— we need to get the feel of drawing on pavement."

"But we should pick some out-of-the-way

place, so people don't see our practice draw-ings."

"How about the alley behind the hard-ware store?"

"The alley is good. Let's go."

We dumped our chalks into a shopping bag, along with some stale fig bars for Henrietta, and headed for the alley. We found a good spot, with nice smooth pavement. We got some broken-down cardboard boxes to kneel on, divided up the chalks, and picked a space for each of us to work in.

Then Bruno Ugg said, "I don't know what to draw!"

"Neither do I," I said.

"I can think of things to draw," Loretta Fischetti said. "But I don't know what to draw for the contest. I mean, I don't suppose any of us will win—but we ought to try. What sort of picture would be good for a contest entry?"

None of us had any idea.

"We could ask Lucy Casserole for sugges-tions," I said.

"No! Then she might think we were weenies. Besides she's one of the judges. We can't ask a judge what we should draw."

"We can't ask Hilangully Ryder, the only other artist we know—assuming we could find him," Loretta Fischetti said. "He's a judge too."

"And a contestant," I said.

"And he might call us finger wigglers," Bruno Ugg said. "We need to ask someone who is impartial."

"And likes us," Loretta Fischetti said.

"And knows a lot," I said.

"To the library! To the library!" we all shouted.

XXXII

"**S**o, you want to know what subjects are suitable for an art competition," Starr Lackawanna said.

"Of course, we don't expect to win," Loretta Fischetti said.

"But it would be cool if we did," Bruno Ugg said.

"I am planning to do a drawing myself," Starr Lackawanna said. "I will draw this library building."

"So, you don't expect to win either," Bruno Ugg said.

"I just want to participate, and publicize the library," Starr Lackawanna said. "But it so happens, I did create a list of winning pictures in civic art contests in New Jersey for the past ten years."

"May we see the list?" I asked.

"Yes, you may, or I can tell you what sort of pictures tended to do well in the contests," Starr Lackawanna said.

"What sort?" we asked.

"Patriotic pictures, and ones about American history, won in a majority of contests," Starr Lackawanna said. "Pictures of George Washington and Abraham Lincoln, flags, American eagles."

"Ohhh! Eagles," Loretta Fischetti said. "I'm going to do an eagle."

"Abraham Lincoln! I like Lincoln!" I said. "I will do a picture of old Honest Abe."

"I will do my own version of Washington crossing the Delaware," Bruno Ugg said.

"The library can lend you books with pictures of those subjects, and you may also check out prints, including one of the painting of Washington crossing the Delaware by Emanuel Gottlieb Leutze," Starr Lackawanna said. "By the way, did you know that Vic Trola is back from visiting his mother, and

WRJR, the pirate radio station, is on the air starting today?"

"Cool," Loretta Fischetti said. "I'll get my portable radio, and we can listen while we practice our drawings in the alley."

XXXIII

Before Vic Trola went off the air to go visit his mother, we always listened to the radio, usually while reading. When he wasn't there, we refrained from listening to regular radio stations—out of loyalty, I guess.

When we were set up in the alley again, this time with Loretta Fischetti's radio playing, we felt really in the groove. Vic Trola was playing an all-day retrospective of all the recordings of the Ugly Bug Blues-and-Klezmer Band. It was great music, and we sort of bounced up and down, kneeling on our pieces of cardboard boxes as we worked on our drawings.

Working from the books Starr Lackawanna had let me check out of the library, I got a pretty good portrait of Mr. Lincoln down. Anyway, I thought it was good for a first try. I drew him in his stovepipe hat, which I have always liked. With the hat, it didn't look so much like the picture on the five-dollar bill. Then I added red and white stripes, like the American flag, across the picture behind him. Bruno Ugg and Loretta Fischetti liked my drawing.

Loretta Fischetti's eagle was excellent. It had its beak open and a wild look in its eye. She copied my flag stripes, only hers were sort of loopy instead of straight across.

Bruno Ugg got into trouble with his Washington crossing the Delaware. He stayed pretty close to the print Starr Lackawanna had checked out to him—and the problem was getting all the people in. It wound up looking like a boat with this huge dark clump in it—like a pile of stuff, dirt or bricks or something. We suggested he try leaving some of the people out.

"We should come back tomorrow and practice in another part of the alley," Loretta Fischetti said. We had been there all afternoon, and didn't realize it until we got hungry.

"Let's start in the morning," I said.

"Bring the radio again," Bruno Ugg said.

XXXIV

We got an early start the next morning. We found another good spot, farther up the alley.

"Look at this!" Bruno Ugg said. "Someone's been drawing here already!"

There was a drawing on the pavement, and it was a lollapalooza. It was like colored lightning. There were flashes of orange and yellow, and a bright electric green. It wasn't of anything—it was abstract, like some of our collages. And it sure was good.

"This rocks," Loretta Fischetti said.

"Someone must have been up at the crack of dawn, drawing this," I said.

"Or they drew it at night," Bruno Ugg said. "See? There's a street lamp above."

"Could this be someone else practicing for the contest, like we are? Do you think

this could be one of Lucy Casserole's?" I asked.

"It's possible," Bruno Ugg said. "But it's sort of funky and wild for Lucy Casserole."

"Maybe it's by Hilangully Ryder," Loretta Fischetti said. "We don't know what his stuff looks like."

"But Hilangully Ryder is all intellectual," I said. "Remember all that 'use your loaf' stuff he was talking about? This doesn't look like somebody thought about it, or planned anything. It looks like someone just went nuts with the chalks."

"It's a heck of a picture," Bruno Ugg said.

"Let's get to work," Loretta Fischetti said. "With stuff like this in the contest, we'd better come up with good art, or people will say we're finger wigglers."

"I'm going to make my American flag stripes orange and yellow this time," I said.

"I think I'll put a setting sun behind the boat," Bruno Ugg said.

"I need to make the eagle's claws bigger," Loretta Fischetti said.

"I sort of like the finger wiggling," I said.

"I do too," Loretta Fischetti said. "But we don't want to appear uncool."

We made progress in our second day of practice. We spent the whole morning in the alley, drawing and listening to Vic Trola play old cowboy songs and delta blues.

We went home for a quick lunch and a bottle of Dr. Pedwee's grape.

"Where's Henrietta? I haven't seen her all day," Bruno Ugg asked.

"I bet she's hanging out at Vic Trola's radio station," I said. "You know, she used to be his chicken, and he's been away. She likes to visit him sometimes."

When we returned to the alley for more practice, there was another of those wild abstract drawings.

"Wow! The mad artist came back here and knocked out another one while we were having lunch!" I said.

"And we missed finding out who it is," Bruno Ugg said.

"I bet we find out tomorrow," Loretta Fischetti said. "At the contest."

XXXV

There was a pretty decent turnout in front of City Hall, considering that Meehan the Bum had organized the event. The mayor was there, so were Lucy Casserole, Davis Davisdavis, and Hilangully Ryder. Vic Trola was there—he had set up a microphone and was broadcasting live coverage of the art contest. Also Professor Mazzocchi, who had created Henrietta, was there—and Henrietta was there. Professor Mazzocchi was petting her. Starr Lackawanna was there. My parents, Bruno Ugg's parents, and Loretta Fischetti's parents were there. There was a little crowd of people ready to take part in the contest, mostly kids, milling around.

This was how the contest worked. Each

artist signed his or her name on a sheet of paper, and Meehan the Bum handed over a box of chalks. Then we were each assigned an address on Washington Street—various merchants had agreed to allow a drawing to be made in front of their stores and to wash the drawing off on Monday morning. At 11:00 A.M., the judges would walk along Washington Street, view all the pictures, and pick winners. Then there would be a ceremony in front of City Hall, certificates would be awarded, and there would be free hot dogs and soda. For the rest of Saturday, and all day Sunday, citizens could walk along Washington Street and enjoy the art.

The mayor made a speech about the long and glorious artistic tradition in Hoboken, and he thanked the North Hoboken Social and Athletic Club for paying for the free hot dogs and sodas.

Then Meehan the Bum spoke. "Hello, ladies and gentlemen and would-be artists. I am Pierpont Meehan, official organizer of this competition and exhibit. Even though this city has a Democratic adminstration, your elected officials have seen fit to authorize this spectacular expression of creativity. This outpouring of art will bring enlightenment and happiness to the people of Hoboken. We are going to award prizes—but remember, it is about the art. Those of you who wind up being losers should not feel badly just because you are inferior to the artists who receive recognition and get their names in the paper. Just have fun, and if your drawing stinks, it only means that you have no talent, not that you are a bad person. And now ... let the games begin!"

We had our assignments. Mine was in front of Carl's House of Hats. Bruno Ugg's position was a few doors down, in front of Tommy's Salamis. Loretta Fischetti was in the next block, in front of the Hebrew Sons of Ireland meeting hall. Starr Lackawanna and Hilangully Ryder were somewhere on the other side of the street. I could see Henrietta way up the street, shuffling around, dancing or kicking garbage probably.

On either side of me were two little kids, who were already hard at work on little-kid drawings, the kind showing a house with a curl of smoke coming out of the chimney, a yellow sun in the sky, a couple of birds, and people drawn with their arms sticking out to the sides. These two wouldn't be much competition.

I figured Hilangully Ryder would probably nab first prize. He was a professional artist. I thought it wasn't quite fair for him to compete. And he was a judge, too. Since almost all the contestants were younger than us, it seemed to me that Bruno Ugg, Loretta Fischetti, and I had a good shot at winning second, third, and fourth place.

I knew it was really about the art, and that I shouldn't feel competitive. Still, I wanted people to think the members of the Artsy Smartsy Club were good artists. I didn't want them to think we were just ordinary kids or finger wigglers.

XXXVI

I got to work on Mr. Lincoln. At first I felt a little nervous, drawing right on Washington Street, with people walking past and some of them stopping to watch me work. Some of them made comments to each other, or asked me questions like, "Who's that supposed to be? Lincoln?" But as the drawing began to take shape, I got more and more involved and was hardly aware of anything else. I guess that's how a real screever feels. I wasn't thinking much about the people, or the kids working on either side, or even that I was in a contest.

I must have worked on my drawing for two hours, after which I had chalked everything, including the buttons on Mr. Lincoln's coat. I straightened up and looked at it. It was good. "I think it's finished," I said.

I walked over to see how Bruno Ugg's picture was coming along. He was standing up, brushing chalk off his clothes. His drawing was finished too. He had done a good job.

"Nice," I said. "I like the way you did the water. Come see mine."

Bruno Ugg said he thought my drawing was better than his.

"No, yours is better. That setting sun is really great."

"Let's see what Loretta Fischetti drew," Bruno Ugg said.

Loretta Fischetti's eagle was really incredible. It was dramatic. We were impressed with the way she did every feather. Then, of course, Loretta had to walk back with us and see our pictures. She said that both of our drawings were better than hers.

Then we walked up one side of Washington Street, checking out everybody else's drawing. Some of the little kids had done pretty good work—but they had long since finished and were now milling around in front of City Hall, pushing each other and running up and down, waiting for the free hot dogs.

Hilangully Ryder's picture was surprising. He had printed the title under it: *Moonless Night and Fog in the North Atlantic*. It was completely black, with maybe a little purple.

"That's really what it looks like out there, kiddies," Hilangully Ryder said. "Look and learn."

Starr Lackawanna's drawing of the library building was very neatly done. We all complimented her.

We crossed Washington Street and started back down, intending to look at the pictures on that side.

The first one made us stop in our tracks.

It was wild. It had corn muffins that Van Gogh might have painted, a Bellini sky, and St. Francis giving potato chips to a chicken. There were streaks and stripes of yellow, orange, and pale green—and a bowl full of tennis balls. Crouching in the corner was

Meehan the Bum, done in a Cubist style and wearing the red robes of St. Jerome in the El Greco painting.

"Holy Toledo!" Bruno Ugg said. "Who do you suppose did this one?"

"The mad artist! It's like a double lolla-palooza!" Loretta Fischetti said.

"Here come da judges," I said. "If this drawing doesn't get first prize, I'm a walrus."

XXXVII

Koo koo ka choo! Chaos broke out in front of City Hall. To begin with, the free hot dogs and soda had not arrived, and the crowd was starting to grumble. Then, Hilangully Ryder insisted his picture, *Moonless Night and Fog in the North Atlantic*, had to win first prize.

None of the other judges agreed with him.

"You are know-nothings, philistines, and goo-goos!" Hilangully Ryder shouted at the other judges.

"Why is he a judge?" the mayor asked. "How can he be a contestant and a judge? That is irregular. It smacks of corruption. We do not do things like that in Hoboken."

"Where are the free hot dogs?" someone in the crowd shouted.

"Free hot dogs! Free hot dogs!" people in the crowd began to chant.

"Free hot dogs! Free all political prisoners!" Meehan the Bum shouted.

"What political prisoners?" the mayor asked. He raised his hands and shouted to the crowd, "The city of Hoboken has no political prisoners. We have no prisoners of any kind."

"What about the hot dogs?" the crowd shouted.

"We have no hot dogs of any kind either," the mayor shouted back. "I don't know what happened. Let's get on with the awarding of prizes. I'm sure the hot dogs will turn up."

"My picture gets first prize!" Hilangully Ryder shouted.

"You are out-voted," Meehan the Bum said.

"You are disqualified!" the mayor shouted.

"I protest!" Hilangully Ryder shouted.

"Your protest is moot!" the mayor shouted.

"What does moot mean?" Bruno Ugg asked.

"I refuse to be mooted!" Hilangully Ryder said. "I am going to lie down in the middle of the street as an expression of protest."

"If you lie down in the middle of the street, you will endanger public safety, and I will have you taken into custody!" the mayor shouted.

Hilangully Ryder marched into the middle of Washington Street and lay down.

"Officer Spooney," the mayor said. "Take two men and lay hands on that man."

Officer Spooney and two other policemen lifted Hilangully Ryder and carried him into City Hall.

"I am a political prisoner," Hilangully Ryder shouted to the crowd.

"Free political prisoners! Free the crazy guy! Free hot dogs!" the crowd shouted.

XXXVIII

That was not the end of the chaos.

Next came the selection of prizewinners by the remaining judges.

Lucy Casserole and Davis Davisdavis wanted to give first prize to the wild picture Bruno Ugg, Loretta Fischetti, and I had been so impressed with. The one we thought was by the Mad Artist.

But Meehan the Bum pointed out that the location of the picture, in front of Sven's Vegetable Market, was not an official location—and as far as his records showed, it had not been done by a properly registered contestant.

"But it is a great drawing," Lucy Casserole said. "It is a syncretic and partially abstract work, with homages to Bellini, Van Gogh, and El Greco, and you yourself are included in the picture."

"That does not matter," Meehan the Bum said. "As the organizer of this cultural event, I am an official of the city of Hoboken. I represent civic order."

"You are a bum!" Lucy Casserole said. "You spend every day in the public park, drinking wine out of a paper bag!"

"Mr. Mayor," Meehan the Bum asked the mayor. "Is there a law against insulting a public official?"

"You are not a public official," the mayor said. "And, no. People insult me all the time."

"Where are the hot dogs?" the crowd shouted.

"I demand you put this woman in jail," Meehan the Bum said to the mayor.

"No," the mayor said. "Besides, I never heard her insult you."

"She called me a bum," Meehan the Bum said.

"You are a bum," the mayor said. "That's

describing, not insulting."

"He's also a numbskull," Lucy Casserole said.

"You heard that!" Meehan the Bum said to the mayor. "Have her arrested."

"Let's get done with voting for winners," the mayor said. "If the hot dogs don't arrive soon, this crowd will rush us."

"Then I demand Lucy Casserole and Davis Davisdavis change their votes," Meehan the Bum said. "They should choose a picture by a duly registered contestant."

"We will not change our votes," Davis Davisdavis said.

"We chose the best picture," Lucy Casserole said.

"I can solve this," the mayor said. "Will the artist who did the picture with the corn muffins and the saints and all that please step forward."

No one stepped forward but Henrietta, who gave the mayor a little affectionate peck on the cheek.

"I repeat, will the person who did the

syncretic abstract whatever-it-is, with the portrait of Meehan the Bum, please come forward," the mayor said.

The four judges and Henrietta were standing on the City Hall steps, facing the crowd.

"Last call," the mayor said. "If the artist does not present him- or herself, we will disqualify the entry."

The mayor was waving the first-prize certificate in his hand. The guy from the *Jersey Journal* had his camera ready to take a picture of the mayor handing the certificate to the winner.

Someone in the crowd shouted, "Look! The hot dogs!"

Far up Washington Street, two sweating fat guys in suits from the North Hoboken Social and Athletic Club were pushing a hot dog cart, the kind with the little umbrella on top. The umbrella was wobbling.

"The hot dogs! The hot dogs!" the crowd chanted. "Free hot dogs!"

The crowd took a step, as one person, toward the wobbling umbrella. Then it took another step. Then it began to surge toward the umbrella.

"Wait!" the mayor shouted. "The prizes!"

The crowd began to run.

The sweating fat guys in suits looked scared.

Davis Davisdavis shoved certificates into the hands of the members of the Artsy Smartsy Club. "Here, kids. Second, third, and fourth place. Congratulations," he said.

The guy from the *Jersey Journal* snapped a picture.

"Hot dogs! Hot dogs! Free hot dogs!" the crowd shouted as it ran up Washington Street.

The crowd met up with the sweating fat guys in suits in the middle of the block between First and Second Streets. The sweating fat guys in suits panicked and ran the other way.

That was when the clap of thunder happened. And the lightning. And the intense cloudburst. Rain came down in buckets. The sky got dark as night. In a second we were soaking wet. The mayor was wet. He gave a little yelp and ducked into City Hall. Lucy Casserole was wet. Davis Davisdavis was wet. Henrietta was running like the wind down Washington Street in the direction of our houses.

The sidewalks along Washington Street were a swirl of color as the rain erased the First Annual Hoboken Street Art Festival and Competition. In the middle of the block between First and Second Streets, many hot dogs were washed into the sewers along with all the creativity.

People scurried into doorways, those who had reached the cart first holding hot dogs on soggy buns.

From within City Hall, we heard the voice of Hilangully Ryder shouting, "It's a judgment! This is what you all deserve for disrespecting great art!"

There was no point in running. We were soaked through and through. The Artsy Smartsy Club walked the block to our buildings, carrying our wet certificates.

XXXIX

We went to our respective homes to towel off and put on dry things. Then we appeared, one by one, in the basement, each with wet clothes to stuff in the dryer.

Henrietta was perched on the old couch, asleep, with her feathers fluffed out, smelling like a soggy chicken.

"Quite a day," I said.

"Yep," Bruno Ugg said.

"Lots of excitement," Loretta Fischetti said.

"I wonder who did that drawing," I said.

"I wonder too," Bruno Ugg said.

"I also wonder," Loretta Fischetti said.

We sat there in the basement, listening to the dryer, wondering.

While we wondered, we looked at Henrietta, sleeping peacefully, all fluffed out, drying and smelling soggy. She looked happy. She looked as though she were smiling—if a chicken can smile.

"Do you see what she's holding in her claw?" Loretta Fischetti asked.

"I was just noticing that," Bruno Ugg said.

"Piece of paper," I said.

"It looks like . . ."

It was. It was the First Prize certificate.

"No doubt she snatched it out of the mayor's hand when the thunderstorm hit," Bruno Ugg said.

"No doubt," Loretta Fischetti said.

"Just a reflex, I suppose," I said.

"No doubt," Bruno Ugg said.

"She seems to have some colored chalk on her feathers," Loretta Fischetti said.

"Well, there was a lot of chalk around," I said.

"Yes," Bruno Ugg said.

"Yes," Loretta Fischetti said.

We looked at one another.

"It's not possible, is it?" Bruno Ugg said.

"Well, it's possible," Loretta Fischetti said.

"She's a very unusual chicken," I said.

"Yes," Bruno Ugg said.

"She is," Loretta Fischetti said.

"So what shall we do, tack our certificates up on the wall?" Bruno Ugg asked.

"Good idea. Let's do that," Loretta Fischetti said.

"Including Henrietta's?" I asked.

"Sure, why not?"